MW00879096

WORD WEAVERS

SAGE OUTLAW WRITER

BOOK 4

TABLE OF CONTENTS

FORWARD

The Sage Outlaw Writers first published in 2019 when Bonnie Lyons was the facilitator. She created an atmosphere that engendered community. She participates as a writer and as an editor. Thank you, Bonnie.

Since then, the group has lost members and gained new ones. Janie Alonso has generously become our facilitator. We are grateful for her support.

We thank the Alicia Trevino Senior Center for allowing us to meet in their facilities. Without their support, we would have disbanded.

Our work is made up of personal memoirs, recommended writing prompts, and ten-word challenges, identified by the underlining of the words assigned. We choose forms from essays to narratives to poems.

We continue to learn through our writings and discussions. Sharing our work in a book for others to read encourages us to write carefully. We enjoy the process. Hopefully, you will too.

JANIE ALONSO

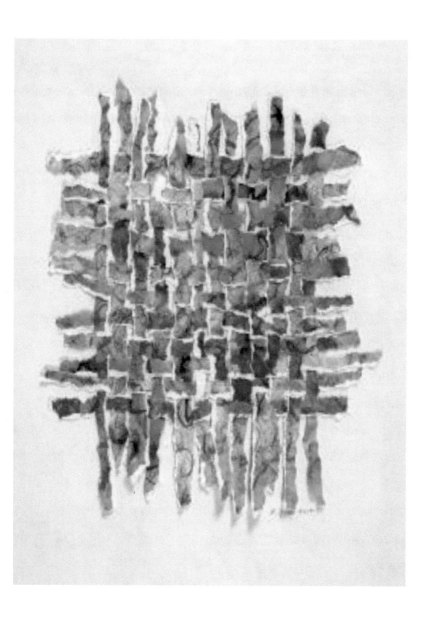

HURTFUL WORDS

It was 1966 and I was in middle school 7th grade. My physical education teacher hooked her finger and motioned for me to come to her side. She wrinkled her nose saying, "You don't smell very nice. I want you to shower today," I had just finished running around the gym with other classmates. All I could say was, "Yes, Ma'am" We were not allowed to talk back to teachers.

I would have liked to explain to her that our house had no hot water. If I wanted to bathe on these cold nights, wood had to be chopped, for a fire to heat up the big seventeen-gallon galvanized tin tub had to be filled with water. There were no inside faucets, so we had to carry buckets of water from the bathroom to fill the tub. This sometimes took hours.

The other problem was the school showers had no privacy. There were no doors or curtains, and they would give us a hand towel to dry ourselves. It was embarrassing showering in front of other girls. We had just started developing breasts and pubic hair. We had seen the movie about our periods in fifth grade, and it never mentioned we would get hair under our arms or our private parts. I envied the girls who would walk around with no shame or inhibition. Being Catholic we were told modesty was a virtue. I showered as fast as I could and changed clothes.

My parents could not afford to buy us deodorant, so I would use my brother's Right Guard spray. It was strong and burned my armpits. But it was better than nothing.

A teacher's words can be hurtful. To this day I worry about how I smell. I don't overdo it with perfume. I wear light smelling lotions. I wash my hair every day and practice good oral hygiene. I don't want anyone to ever tell me I smell bad.

UVALDE

My body feels like my wings have been pulled off, slowly.
My iridescent purple appendages of creativity and lightness are lying on the ground.
I feel defeated, broken, my hopeful spirit on the verge of extinction.
My mind is with the children whose lives have evaporated in the hot Texas sun.
My soul cries out for justice.
Anger and sadness crush together.
A purge of wailing has not completed the healing process.
We release tears and anger.
Otherwise, we will not see with eyes of clarity.
We have relentless work to do, and we will not forget.
We *cannot* forget.
A profound change is necessary for our souls and the souls of children.

THE JOY OF HOUSEKEEPING (A FAIRY TALE)

Cheerful is the woman who wakes up before her family to cook breakfast

Praise the biscuits rising flaky and buttery from her hands

Praise her as she bids a cheerful goodbye to her children and husband

Praise the dirt and grime swept daily with happy twirls of her straw broom

Praise the wet mop swishing back and forth dancing like waves on a beach

Praise the tousled beds stripped to bare mattresses

Praise the stench of toilets which require masks and gloves to cleanse the foulness of bodily functions.

Praise as pine-scented breezes linger in the bathroom

Praise the stinky laundry in a hamper that overflows onto the floor, an eruption of socks and soiled underwear

Praise the breakfast, lunch and dinner dishes and pots we use to prepare meals

Those caked-on eggs, macaroni and cheese and grease give smiles to the manual dishwasher

Praise be the dust as it attaches itself like a Saharan storm to everything

Praise the woman who makes time to change into a dress, high heels, and pearls to please a husband who has worked hard all day

Indeed, it is a fairy tale.

WHAT FEW PEOPLE KNOW ABOUT ME

A song in elementary school "The Bear went over the mountain" was a favorite of mine. He wanted to see what was on the other side of the mountain. This was my first taste of wanderlust. I wanted to see everything, especially snow-capped mountains, wide rolling rivers, sandy beaches with turquoise water, giant Sequoia trees and lush green valleys.

I would have to keep moving because I got bored easily. I believe that is what happened in my marriage. I kept learning by going to college, reading, visiting museums and other extracurricular activities. He was happy watching television, smoking cigarettes, and drinking coffee. We had nothing to talk about.

I remember watching a movie about the aborigines in Australia and their walkabouts. They would take a foot journey in order to live in a more traditional manner. It seemed so natural to wander around the country. I believe people who are living the "van" life have the same type of wanderlust. If I won a large lottery, I would buy a good recreational vehicle, and I would be off. I would travel to all the National and state natural parks throughout the United States. Texas alone has eight-nine state parks, with the Big Bend Natural Area being the largest. My family and I enjoyed nature at Big Bend in the nineteen nineties and the sky was the clearest blue I have ever seen. Washington and Oregon are known for their natural parks and Mt. Rainer is my favorite.

When I was in high school my brother had a book about survival. I read it from beginning to end in one night. It described a monster in the great northwest called Bigfoot. I was hooked. It was hard to find books or any literature on this elusive creature back in the seventies. If I want to hear or read stories about Sasquatch today, I will just search YouTube. I enjoy hearing the stories. Some are fictional and some are told as facts. I believe it is possible they do exist. I am fascinated; however, please note the following: I don't want to see one, hear one, smell one or search for one. If I did see one, I would wet and poop my pants. Many men have written that they can't control their fear and their bodies lose control. I believe it to be true.

One thing people don't know is I like to surround myself with people who like to read, write, paint, and research current events. The energy from everyone continues to light a flame of my eternal quest for an intriguing life.

DIA DE LOS FINADOS NOVEMBER 2, 2022,
ALL SOULS DAY

Every year on November 2nd is Dia de Los Finados or All Souls Day. We would visit the Santa Rosa cemetery in Melchor Muzquiz Coahuila Mexico. Unlike the city cemeteries in the United States, the cemetery in Muzquiz was not kept up. It was up to families to tend to the plots of their deceased loved ones. We would have to clear all the overgrown weeds to get to the grave sites. Con machetes the brush would be cleared, and gravestones were washed and cleaned. The ones with crosses had to be replaced with new fresh white paint.

My mother and father would take us children to visit our grandfathers' plots. This part of Mexico is dusty and dry. There was always swirling dirt to cover our shoes and clothes. We began early in the morning. My grandmothers would go with us to help in any way they could. Abuelita Mela was a petite, dark-skinned India with braided hair. I remember she rolled her own Bugler cigarettes and smoked like a chimenea. She was always dressed in black from head to toe to signify she was a widow. Abuelita Virginia was tall, blue eyed, husky, and strong. She was a good storyteller and kept us occupied.

Being an older child, I would listen to my Abuelita Virginia tell her stories of the giant snake that lived underneath the tombs. It roamed underneath the earth looking for fresh cadavers that had no coffins. Yes, some people were poor and could only afford a wrapping of linen on their bodies. She had our full attention when she told us about the young girl who had found a small egg in a field. She placed it in her mouth and was running with her school friends and swallowed the egg by accident. She thought nothing of it and didn't tell her parents. A few days later she fell ill, and the country doctor could not find any reason for her pain and fevers. She died the next day and when an autopsy was performed, baby snakes had hatched in her insides and had eaten her guts. Ayyy Cucuy!!!!

"A trabajar," someone yelled. Our break with Abuela stopped and we went back to work.

My Mom and Dad each had ten brothers and sisters, and some were deceased. There were still a lot of graves to clean.

As the evening stars appeared, their light competed with the blaze of candles on the plots. Favorite songs were sung such as Cien Años, La Media Vuelta, Cucurucucu Paloma, songs of the Golden Era.

It was time to go to our abuelita Virgina's house for our meal and memories of our Finados.

Now Los Finados are Gilbert and Victoria Alonso, Alejandro Alonso, Jose Luis Alonso and Oscar Alonso, my parents, and brothers.

WE REGRET TO INFORM YOU

I was twelve years old when my brother Oscar joined the Marines right after graduation in May 1966. The Vietnam war was front and center in our daily lives. Every night at 6 pm, the national news was televised, and Walter Cronkite provided all the latest information. We would watch the newscast on our black and white television set. The reports ended in silence. A roll call of the name of every person lost in Vietnam either KIA (Killed in Action) or MIA (Missing in Action) scrolled on the TV screens in large black letters.

My brother voluntarily enlisted in the Marines without my parents' consent. His first airplane ride was to California where he was stationed at Camp Pendleton for basic training. According to his letters, it was a grueling six weeks of physical fitness, rifle training and hand to hand combat. He graduated and got a medal for being a marksman. He would send us letters and pictures. It felt like he was a million miles away.

Soon after he got his orders to go to Vietnam. My Mom started praying for his safe return. She counted the days until his tour was completed. She would not allow avocados or watermelon into the house if he was gone. They were his favorite foods, and this was her way of keeping good thoughts about his safe return.

Every evening, I looked for my brother's name on that roll call hoping and praying his name would not be on that list.

We heard at school a letter would be sent if someone was killed with the words; "We regret to inform you" No one ever wanted to receive a letter with those regrets.

When he returned to the United States after two tours, he had served his time and did not re-enlist.

It was a late Friday night in 1971 when he arrived safely home. My Mom and Dad knew he was returning; however, they didn't tell us. I remember staying up until the next morning as he told us all about Vietnam. The people he said were just as poor as us and he felt comfortable with them. He learned to eat what they ate, which was rice and fish. He learned to speak Vietnamese and was an asset in interrogations. He brought us presents from his stopover in Taiwan and Thailand. He had bought some sharkskin suits which were the fashion rage at that time. To this day my sister-in-law still has them in her closet. A complete set of encyclopedias arrived later, and we were elated.

My brother went to sleep later that first morning. It wasn't until the afternoon Mom realized he had slept on the bare floor; he had become accustomed to the hard surface. He had changed both physically and mentally. My brother never talked about the deaths he saw in Vietnam. It wasn't until years later, he shared stories of his friends who had died in combat and others who had been killed. Even after he returned, the names continued to roll call on our living room television. Thankfully I didn't have to look for his name anymore.

CHILDHOOD TERRORS

Did I ever tell you I grew up in a bitterly cold, drafty house in the country? The cheaply made three-bedroom home was in the middle of two dirt roads. The wooden sidings hung loosely like rotting teeth. After the sun went down, wood rats invaded our home as easily as Attila the Hun. Because there was no insulation between the walls and sheetrock, they roamed freely, wild horses on the plains. The pitter patter of hundreds of clawed feet was terribly noisy in the naked roof and walls. They were hungry, wolves looking for a quick meal. The first winter we lost bread, beans, rice, even soap to starving, unruly, hairy critters. They angrily fought each other for every scrap. They would fight like junkyard dogs. Bodies slamming together like wrestlers in a ring. Sometimes angry screeching was heard, another rat was killed and cannibalized. It was terrifying trying to sleep. When the wind shook the windows, you would swear rattlesnakes were nearby. We would wake up in the bitter cold house our breath like white cotton candy clouds. Sometimes we had heat from a lone gas heater. Because of the drafts we had to stand in front of them hoping we would not burn our butts and have purple welts. Our gas came from a butane tank outside. When there was no money to buy fuel, it would be a cold week. Dad would chop wood and

17

burn it in a fire pit. The red-hot embers would be collected with a shovel and placed in a bucket. The buckets were carried and placed in the living room. We sat around but it didn't work. The house was forever drafty and would not release its cold grip. The rats came whether it was freezing cold or not.

STARTING OVER

His picture on the on-line dating website, Finding True Love Inc., grabbed her attention. He was wearing a charcoal-colored fedora tilted sideways like a movie screen idol from the forties. He had a twinkle in his dark brown eyes beckoning her to seek him out. She was entranced by his burnt sienna skin that was peeping out his crisp, open button-down white shirt. His mustache gave her a twinge in her heart she had not felt in a long time. This was the man of her Turner Classic Movies dreams, a mix of Clark Gable, William Holden and Cary Grant.

June Marie always thought she had been born in the wrong era. She loved to wear dresses with high heels and matching short gloves when she could find them. People in their thirties and forties dressed for simple occasions like dinner. She knew she stood out when she dressed to the "nines" because everyone else wore shorts and t-shirts. Even though she dressed from bygone eras, she was a successful woman with her own business. She used all the technology and business ideas from this millennium. This didn't stop her from fantasizing about starting over in a new place. This man on the website gave her hope.

She read his information carefully reviewing every word. He was looking for a woman who had the same interests, reading, hiking, traveling, museums and watching classic movies. He had to be the one for her. Kismet had sent him her way. She contacted him online and gave her information to him. She could not wait to hear his reply.

It was the following day she got a voicemail message, could you send me your phone number so we can talk? She gladly gave him her number. He called her that evening. He introduced himself and his voice was smooth and deep. She could listen to him all day. They talked for about two hours and had to close early as there was a big difference as he was living in London for his work. He was a commodities trader and would be there for three months. He was from Chicago, Illinois and was tired of being alone. He wanted to find a wife whom he could share his life with. These were the words she had been wanting to hear all her life. It was if she had known him forever. They said good night and the calls came every day in the evening. They were the highlight of her day.

It was four weeks into their relationship when he asked her to fly out to meet him. He would be paying for her round trip and money was no problem. She felt like an heiress who had been given money to travel anywhere. She said yes, she would love to. He would make all the arrangements and contact her soon with the details. She was on a cloud; dreams did come true. She was willing to start over anywhere with him, New York, Paris, Rome, Dubai anywhere!

The following week, she did not hear from him. This was her first red flag. By Friday afternoon, she had an uneasy feeling in the pit of her stomach. She got a text from him in the evening. He had been arrested in London as he had befriended an acquaintance at work. This person had planted drugs in his apartment, and someone had alerted the police. He begged her to be patient with him. He wanted to see her however his assets were frozen, and he knew no one who could help him. He could not call her from jail. He would be so grateful if she could wire him two-thousand dollars so he could post bail.

June Marie's alarm bells went off in her mind. She had seen enough movies where the unsuspecting, naïve, infatuated woman was swindled by a handsome, sweet-talking man. She had fallen for a con artist. Instead of crying she got angry. She texted him back.

Darling, I have missed your silky voice lulling me to sleep. It is terrible news about your incarceration. You have never asked me about my finances before. I am as poor as a church mouse. I live from paycheck to paycheck. I have never seen two thousand dollars in my life. You will have to get that money out of your behind because this pigeon has no money. I am changing my phone number and my life. I am starting over, and you are not invited. And frankly Scarlett, I don't give a damn!!!!

FOLDED PRAYERS

As I heard the phone ringing in my workout bag, I grimaced, *now what!!! Can't I get a moment of peace?*

I wiped the sweat from my forehead and picked it up on the last ring. Teri's calm voice was asking me to help clean the church, on Saturday. She was the president of the Altar Society at Holy Family Church. Yes!!! Something easy, I said to myself. *Sure, I can help*, I answered happily. She continued, *"Also, when are you going to pick up the money?"*

I looked inside my head for an answer, and the chalkboard was blank. *Think, think, think! What money is she talking about?*

Dates, and times, bounced around inside the gray matter that once was my brain. Her voice reached into the corners of my empty skull. *"Janie, the money for the candles?"* My mind echoed with the sound of a long beeeeeeeeeeeeep. There was nothing but a straight line. I imagined Teri in a doctor's uniform placing the defibrillating paddles on my scalp. As she jumpstarted my brainwaves she said, *"You need to pick up the money for the votive candles."*

With embarrassment, I said, *"Oh, my God, I forgot to collect the money. Teri, I will do it as soon as I get out of here."*

As I hung up the phone, I thought to myself, *"Oh great, you took on something else that you can't remember." "Good job, Miss New Treasurer for the Altar Society."* I scolded myself *"Ay tu tu, Miss Treasurer of the Altar Society, el burro sabe mas que tu!"* I still had more whine for that cheese, *" Mas trabajo, don't you have enough to do?*

My demanding schedule of daily workouts at the gym, a 40-hour work week, secretary of the Neighborhood Association, church lector, co-facilitator of our women's meetings, full-time Mom, sister, daughter, aunt, and best friend were leaving me with no time for myself. What I loved doing was making me forgetful, angry, and miserable.

I rushed quickly to the church and gathered all the money from the votive collection boxes. Getting home a few minutes later, I dumped all the money on the kitchen table and knew it was going to take some time to count it all. Letting out a deep sigh, I separated all the change, pennies, dimes, nickels, and quarters into piles. Next, I stacked all the folded dollar bills. There were a lot of them. To no one, I complained, *"This is gonna take all night!"*

In the stillness of the evening, I unfolded each dollar bill and smoothed them so they would be easier to count. With the TV off, I could only hear my breathing and the ticking of the clock. An image of someone folding a dollar bill and inserting it into the collection slot formed inside my head. With hands folded, each bill whispered its prayers.

"Ayudame Dios mio."

"Thank you, Lord, for healing my son."

"Please help me, I feel so alone."

"Diosito mio, ya no aguanto este dolor."

The dollar bills were no longer just pieces of green paper. They were alive with human voices expressing human emotions: fear, despair, grief, joy, happiness, and hope. With my mind open, I listened to what the Lord wanted me to hear. *"Everything you do for me matters. You are important. Thank you for helping me. I've missed you."*

My tears started to fall on the money. I was so busy doing "things" that I had forgotten why I was doing them. All my service was being done with an empty heart.

In all my duties, I had forgotten my relationship with the Lord. My prayers had been put aside for later, when I could get to them, *"I just have to finish this one thing first, Then I promise I will get back to you Lord."* How many times had I promised?

And he waited for me to listen. To hear His voice that was always there if only I sat still and quiet long enough to hear with all my heart and soul. The tears I cried were joyful for I knew that the Lord truly meant what He said. He did miss me, and I missed him.

The distractions of daily life kept me from hearing Him. He was speaking to me through Scripture, sermons, books, and words from friends. I was expecting a howling wind, an earthquake, a flaming fire to catch my attention. The rekindling of my spirit came when I sat at God's feet and heard the still. small voice calling my name to sit beside Him and listen.

LEONARD AMARO

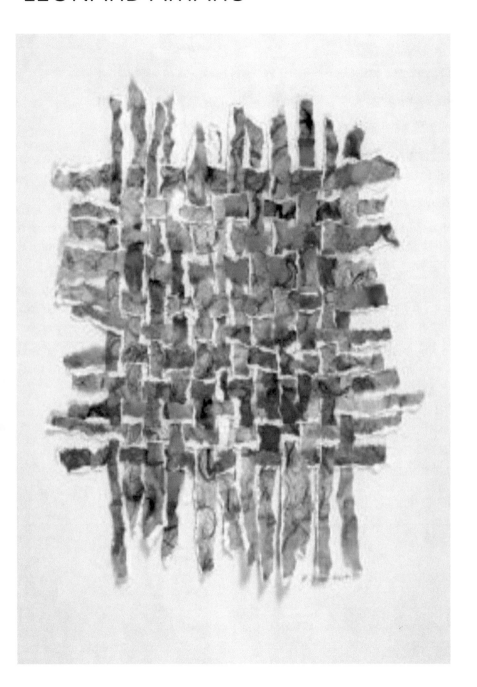

PRAISE

P – pull yourself up, when down – you will now see more clearly!

R – rise above the dark clouds in your life – you will see sunshine!

A – actively seek the best for yourself – you really do deserve it!

I – instantly act important – no mistake - you really are!

S – satisfy yourself with what you have – more is coming your way!

E – enjoy today and everyday – remember, now is the time you have!

We all deserve praise, to receive and to give. It is always better to give then to receive, but humbly accept it when it comes your way. Praise is nourishment to your body, mind, and soul.

You cultivate praise, and it will grow – much will come back to you! Applaud, and be happy for the praise received by other people. The joy and look in their eyes will illuminate back to you, like a star shining down on you.

Praise where you are standing, praise where you are going! Praise will keep the fire within you going. You are a creation with unlimited potential. Praise to that!

MAN IN THE GARAGE

The man sits in his garage watching the world go by. Is he a mechanic, an electrician, a plumber, or simply just an ordinary man sitting in his garage? What can he be thinking? Is he contemplating the tools and materials he may need for his next job? He could simply be having a smoke and a beer – coffee or tea. Sometimes he sits with neighbors or friends, but mostly alone. Not every day do I see him sitting in his garage, but many days yes! Could he be meditating on the day gone by, or the day yet to come? Was the day a hit or a miss? It could be just me wondering what thoughts go through his mind. He usually sets up a small table next to himself. It seems the castle door to his garage is open and ready for war. He must be wondering what all the passersby, either walking or in cars, must be thinking. Those walking their pets, will they pick up the dogs' poop – should it come. Does that man sit in his garage, care what we think, or do we care what he thinks? It must be a way of healing for him and for us to see him sitting in his garage. It is a wonder each day that goes by to catch a glimpse of the man sitting in his garage. One more day of wonderment as each day goes by. The man in the garage gets up, closes the castle garage door. Into his castle he now goes. Into the secret place where only family and close friends know he goes. I am glad just to see him another day. What a wonderful, and sometimes mysterious world we live in. To live another day and see the man in the garage.

COLOR MY DAY

Sunday is a day of worship, a day for rest, and a day of reflection. Sunday is a day to honor our Lord in his Royal Robe. I colored this day - Purple.

Monday is back to school, and to work for many. Maybe, a blah and listless day.

Monday is a day of low energy throughout most of the day. I colored this day-White.

Tuesday is a day of higher energy, and brightness all through the day.

Tuesday – yes, I can accomplish many wonderful things. I colored this day-Yellow.

Wednesday is a day of abundance – a day of high energy most of the day

Wednesday is a highly effective day to do my daily chores. I colored this day - Orange.

Thursday is a calming day for me. My energy level has leveled off. Downward a bit!

Thursday, I may be looking forward to the weekend. I color this day - Blue.

Friday is here, and finally I see payday. Many events are planned for the weekend. I will visit some friends and family. My honey-do list may have to wait. I color this day – Green.

Saturday is a day of fun, and joy with family. There is much love today.

Saturday includes many activities, some planned – most not. I color this day - Red. Leonard C. Amaro

HOMELESS BEATLEA

I am but a homeless ladybug beetle in this great big world of ours.

Free as nature can be, I fly round and round looking for a place to land and rest.

Some say I bring them luck when I land on them.

Red brings not only abundant luck but loads and loads of love.

Yes, this red coat of mine with black spots is like a royal robe.

Know that royalty is not only all around us, but it strives in most of us!

I AM LEONARD OTTO

My name is Leonard Otto, for real, I am the Ot-to one. Ot-to wise I am also known as the rich Juan, who no one really knows. I just thought

I Ot-to let everyone know. I was born on the Ot-to side of the tracks. Now, I own the tracks! I Ot-to needs to tell you, it is fun to be rich. It all happened the Ot-to night when I decided to buy a ticket to win. I did win, and this is the reason for my tale. Ot-to wise, I know you believe this tale of mine. Dust- you all?

I plan to take many trips with my winnings. I have one big Sand-wish in mind. It is to go to the Texas coast and have some fun –Padre-Dise. I have the best of witches for you and hope you can also win the Lotto soon. Antsy this all crazy?

Happy Lotto to all!

I AM - COLORED

I am black – like the lettering on this page – like hot tar pits in a land far away. I am adversities and calamities in our lives which we will overcome.

I am brown – like the ground beneath our feet - like the bark that protects our trees. I am wisdom on this Earth.

I am red – like the magnificent giant trees in our west coast – like the Cardinals that fly through our yard every day. I am courage and love on this Earth.

I am yellow – like sunflowers dancing in the meadows – like ripen bananas on the swaying palm trees. I am happiness and energy on this Earth.

I am blue – like the great big sky up above us – like the seas and oceans all around us. I am trustworthy, and calm on this Earth.

I am white – like the great polar bear up North – like the cold frozen ground in which he walks on. I am cool and bring goodness to this Earth.

I am purple – like ripe plums in the trees, ready to pick – like eggplants ready to harvest. I am wealth and abundance on this Earth.

I am orange – like bright juicy ripe fruit ready to pick from the trees - like the sun high above us. I am joy and success on this Earth. I am green – like the many leaves on many trees – like the lush grass that covers our lawn. I am growth, safety, and security on this Earth.

This world of ours called Earth is of many colors – like an artist's beautiful color wheel – no beginning and no end, round and round it goes.

Yes, the people who inhabit this great Earth are of many colors. Sometimes we are the prime but mostly blended with each other to make us stronger.

Next time, when you see a rainbow across the sky, remember, we are one, but of many colors.

CATNIP DANCE

I live to dance in the great big meadows of this land, or wherever else I might be.

I have been to many gardens dancing to and fro in my beautiful lavender coat.

I sway left and right, and my aroma may be enticing to many feline beasts.

Some say I may drive some feline to dizziness. I say purr-fect!

I must keep dancing to the sounds of nature all around us.

Soon, I could wind up in someone's herbal tea. I can only say Grrrrrrrrrrr!

MAGDA AMARO

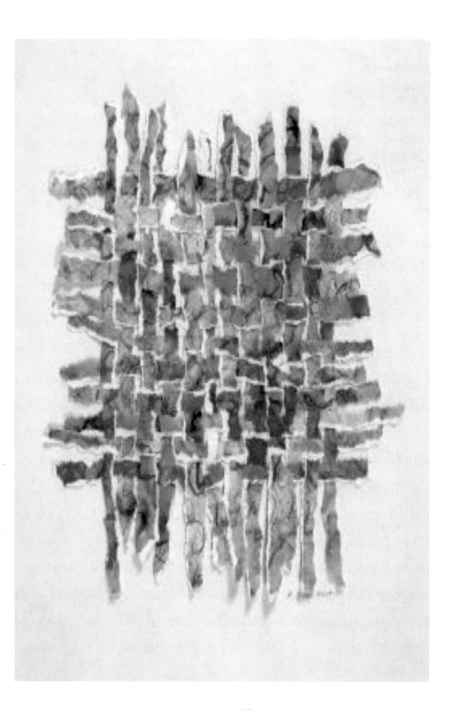

TRAGEDY IN THE BARRIO

She was
> A woman
> A daughter
> A wife
> A mom

The one who held
> The home
> The family
> The marriage
> Always together.

With impeccable behavior and appearance
> Her home was immaculate,
> Her garden perfect
> Her lawn superb
> Her children always looked perfect
> Her husband pressed and starched.

She was always cleaning, keeping herself busy with her housework. Her family included two daughters and one son. Her children always stayed away from others as they were told that they were not like all the kids around them. They were very distant yet quick to look down on any of the kids in the barrio. They would paint themselves as though their clothes were better. Their shoes and their toys were the latest. They acted very snobbishly.

And then it happened.

It was just like any other day. Everyone was awake and off to work or school, yet what happened during that day changed the lives of the whole family, the arrogance of that one proud family, having to accept their mother's death and realization that she had taken her own life. Yet why did she do it? Some say she had a nervous breakdown! Others say that she thought her husband was tired of her and her demands and wanted a divorce. Still others say that the husband had another woman, and she found out.

I was in class with the youngest daughter, but I never found out why or how she took her life. We did find out that they were no longer arrogant or no longer looked down on anybody. I never saw that family again to this day. The barrio was left wounded with a black eye. The women and moms were saddened by her actions for a long time. I always wondered why she did not talk to someone about her problems. I wished that things would have been different for that family.

I often went back to visit weddings and such but never to that barrio. I never saw any of those family members. I was glad to hear from one of my very best friends that they moved to San Antonio. My friend remains friends with one of the family's brothers.

NO SHAME

Well, I have two lovers, and I love them just the same. Now let me tell you about my first lover. He's short and full and only favors the color blue with his green hat. He's always ready to fight. What's that you say? Have you met him? I do not remember what time it was or even the day. Only that he lies right by me as he feels the air with his most powerful scent that only allows me to breathe deeply and sooths my throat and chest. He really does a number on the soles of my feet as he kisses them with smooth strokes and even tickles at times.

Now let me tell you about my second lover. Yes, I often hear someone say, "Magda, how did you meet him?" I met him at the candy store! Yes, there he was standing in his white sports coat and black pants with a red pinstripe shirt. Yes, he is the leader of the pack! He is quite the lover as he caresses my finger with his powerful touch. His warmth penetrates throughout my body. Every part shouts out with attention for his touch. At times, he leaves me wanting more. All my aches escape from my body.

At 75 while I take a sip of my margarita on the rocks since it must be 5pm somewhere, I can say that I have two lovers. What's that fragrance? Is it Versace or Coco Chanel? No! It's Vic and Ben.

NOT MY FIRST KISS

The May of my eighth grade, when school would soon be over, we would say so long to most of the kids with whom I had spent the last three years. Some would be going to private schools. Others would soon enroll in the public school system due to financial needs. Everyone would be going on their own way.

The last week spiraled with many events – graduation, parties, awards banquets luncheons. That first kiss happened at one of those graduation parties.

I always thought it would be so awesome. I would see stars, hear bells or music, my heart full of anticipation. Yet, at that time, I was caught off guard.

I was talking to a boy and turned to pick up another record to put on the record player. When I turned back to face the boy, he was in my face and his lips kissed me.

I could not believe what happened. It was so fast that I was left stunned and with disbelief. That kiss was not a kiss. It was stolen. He was the one who kissed me. I did not kiss him. It was cold, wet, and smeared on my lips. I was not ready for this to happen. Not my FIRST KISS!

And from someone I had known for three years.

I SEE YOU HOMELESS

An observation because I see you, I recall seeing a movie back in the 60s titled, "Running While in the Streets." For the love of San Antonio, no for the love of the human race so I saw her at the corner of West Avenue and Interstate 10. Time has passed and now it's five years later. She is still full of energy and rage. As she stands there, yelling and tearing her clothes off, at times, I start saying prayers for her asking God to please help her and instantly make her whole in her mind and grand in her life. She would be normal and happy with herself; she would be a normal, productive member of society. I remember her five years ago, and still today, I see her and still no help has come to her as she has become invisible to the ones around her like the ordinary San Antonians: mothers, fathers, students, children, etc. invisible to the San Antonio officials like firemen policeman, and district representatives, who ignore her and choose to look the other away. I ask the question, "Have they all been here?" But now today I see so many homeless people out in the streets, both young and old, and I hear on the news that money has been appropriated for the homeless, yet I see many more homeless people in every area of San Antonio. Yes, I see them at the bus stops walking into creeks, hiding in the woods under the freeway in overpasses. I notice how they are surviving, how they manage to exist with their made-up housing, shelter with their wheels to survive and keep going on with their lives day in and day out, and still I see them with their bags of goods, backpacks, suitcases, carts that they use to hold their stuff. Some even have dogs with them as pets. At stores, merchants have posted notices on their doors that say no public restrooms, or restrooms for paying customers only. No restrooms at all. Where are the homeless to bathe?

Where are the homeless to go to the restroom? If they are not allowed access to a restroom, I challenge the City Council to place porta potties throughout the city. Then the homeless may be able to use them and set out the portable shower stalls for the homeless at least once a week for personal hygiene. Yes, San Antonio, you can see the homeless, and you too can do something about it. Will you do it for the love of San Antonio or humanity?

KICKING THE SUMMERTIME BLUES

Sitting around one a Hot Friday afternoon. It was only 3:00p.m., family and friends on the front porch just trying to stay COOL. The front porch just trying to say COOL in the summertime.

It was payday. Someone suggested we go to the coast. Hey! That sounds good!

Yes, Okay Let's do it!

I got gas money!

I have money for food we can cook out on the beach! Okay! Let's meet in an hour already to go!

Cars filled with gas.

Ice, chest filled with meat. OFF to the coast.

We drove three cars on the road to Padre Island.

Once there on the cool beach water swimming and splashing water was a joy.

The sand , the waves and water, it was so relaxing burning our toes in the sand, a wonderful retreat.

E Beach.

Beachside cooking up burgers and hotdogs.

Buns and chips plus soda water.

Everyone gathered round for some food. A cold super sweet slice of watermelon hit the spot for dessert.

Funny how a game of watermelon seeds got started.

The transistor radio was on full blast with the top ten songs we sang along.

A game of volleyball began where anyone could join. Even other beach goers just wanted to play!

Others played a Frisbee toss on the beach!

Night fell, and we sat around telling stories of summers past and all the fun times.

Everyone slept in the cars, some even on the roof of the cars.

In the morning a walk on the beach as we picked-up seashells along the shore.

Morning coffee and orange juice with some Pan duce (sweetbread) for a light breakfast.

Next, say good-bye to Padre Island.

All drivers in agreement. Time to head back to San Antonio.

That spare time trip to the beach was so much fun. A cook-out on the beach side!

Best time to remember! In the summer of '67 on the beach on Padre Island.

JACQUELINE BUTLER

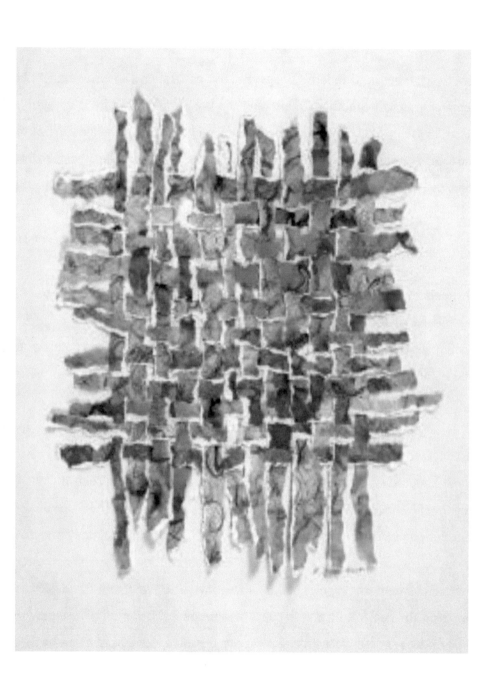

WHAT THIS GENERATION WILL NEVER KNOW

Just imagine all the wonderful things that this generation will never know. Like going to your grandmother's house and the living room furniture is covered in plastic. When you sit on it you slide off. Using the rotary phone, when you pick up the receiver, there's a dial tone, that long cord where you can take the phone into the closet where no one can hear your conversation. Milk being delivered by the milk man.

They will never know the joy of watching the big TV that had that big back end which was the picture tube. TVs then only had three channels to watch. The channels would go off at 12 midnight playing the Star Spangle Banner. You had to get up and go to the TV to change the channels, (no remote), and it was free. Sometimes you had to use wire coat hangers or aluminum foil on the antennas to make the picture come in clearly. Getting up on Saturday morning to watch cartoons.

Going to bed at night and putting your earphones in your ear and listening to your favorite radio station on your transmitter radio. This generation will never know about the assassination of Dr. Martin Luther King, Malcolm X, John F Kennedy his shooter Lee Harvey Oswald who was killed on live TV, by a man named Jack Ruby and Robert Kennedy while making is bid for President. The bus boycott in the 60's when Rosa Park refused to give up her sit to a white person, the civil rights movement, the hippies and their free love. The Watergate scandal, Nixon resigning to keep from being impeached. President Bill Clinton accused of the White House sex scandal with intern Monica Lewinsky, Condoleezza Rice became the first African American to become Secretary of State. The US Space Shuttle

Challenger went up in flames immediately after launch, killing all seven astronauts inside. Nelson Mandela was elected President of South Africa in 1984, The murder of Jon-Benet Ramsey. Still to this day no one has been charged with her murder.

They will never know about the 8 track and the 8-track player that was in cars, then there's the cassette players and how you tried to make a cassette type with all your favorite songs from the radio and the DJ who started talking before the song was over. They will know nothing about going to the library, using the index cards to find the book you're looking for, or the encyclopedia. There's the Metric System which I still have trouble with today. The pay phone that was on almost every street corner. Pencil sharpener on the wall in the classroom, Dial-up Internet, the only one then was AOL, and you couldn't use the phone while someone was on the Internet. The floppy disc where you saved what you had to the computer, today it's a USB drive. Smallpox vaccine scars, of course there's the Oscar Meyer's jingle that got stuck in your head all day.

Before email or texting existed, if you were writing to a friend or family member you did it by hand, a long excruciating process, especially if you had a lot to say. Or you could use a typewriter. The unmistakable clang of the keys pounding on paper. Now you take selfies on your phone. Back in the 60s and 70s you had the photo booth you could find in the malls, you crawled into a cramped little space and waited for the camera to flash three or four times; most of the time you wouldn't like the pictures. Shaking instant Polaroid photos to help them develop faster. Thinking of all the changes that I found would probably become a book. But the last one is my favorite, simply put, there is no need to learn cursive anymore. Perhaps people will still learn it to sign their name, but the days where children spend hours upon hours learning how to write every letter in cursive will be no more.

THE GHOST

Five little girls were lying in a full-size bed late one night talking, laughing and having a good time with not a care in the world. But then they looked toward the door and saw a dark figure standing there. It turned as if it was looking in the room. They thought it was their aunt. She was the aunt of three of the girls and the grandmother of the other two. The oldest of the five asked, "Is that you, auntie?" The figure didn't say a word, just stood there looking at them. At this time all five little girls became afraid and didn't know what to do.

The dark figure turned away from facing the door and started to move toward the living room slowly. The girls looked at one another, got out of bed one at a time and walked to the doorway. They slowly peered around the doorway to see where the dark figure went. To their surprise the figure seemed to be floating into the living room, and they saw it go through the front door. This scared them so much that they ran over each other trying to get back into the bed and pull the covers over their heads. They were so scared they couldn't sleep.

Later that night auntie finally came home. The girls were trying to tell her what had happened, but they were all talking at once, so she couldn't understand a word they were saying. "Calm down" auntie told them when I the oldest told her what that saw, all she did was laugh. "Stop telling that lie." She said, "You know you didn't see no ghost in this house." They told her they thought it was her, but when she walks in the dark house, she has a lit cigarette in her mouth. The girls spent the next two hours trying to convince Auntie what really happened. She even went to the front door to see if it was locked, and it was. "OK, so who do you think it was?" auntie asked them. Well since it wasn't you, it must have been mama, the mother of the three girls, who had died only a few months before, and that is why they were now living with auntie. Til this day they still say that it was their mother who had come to check on them and make sure they were doing alright.

ODE TO SATURDAY MORNING

Oh, Saturday morning, the end of the week
All I want to do is lie between my sheets.
My mother calls me from the kitchen to eat
Oh, Saturday morning. my favorite day of the week
Where I lie in front of the TV, and eat my cereal that is so good to me
Oh, Saturday morning you have my favorite cartoon shows
Bugs Bunny, Road Runner, and the Flintstones and many more
At noon all the cartoons are gone, so it is time for me to do my chores
Clean and vacuum my bedroom and clean the bathroom too
Oh, Saturday morning how I wish you could stay on
Oh, Saturday morning how I long for you right now
Oh, Saturday morning sitting in class thinking of you so dear
I cannot wait to get out of here, then I can go home and go to sleep
So, when I awake, it will be Saturday once again

LETTER TO MY YOUNG SELF

Dear Eleven-year-old me

I wish there was a way you could be the woman I am today without the hurt, but it's not possible I am not sure where to start, I guess I will start with hard stuff first. Next year you will suffer your first great loss: your mother will die after being sick for many years. You and your siblings will go to live temporarily with your aunt and uncle. In a year you and your two sisters will move in with your father and new wife. Four years later he will get sick. You will go to see him on your sixteenth birthday, but two days later he suffers a heart attack and dies. At that time, you are living with your father and new wife. When at home you spend most of your time in your bedroom, so you don't have to deal with your father's wife. You will be treated differently from your sister. All the other losses will only make you stronger and the person you are today.

The vision you have about going to the Air Force after graduation, not going to happen. Don't let it get you down, when people tell you it's your fault when bad things happen to you. Don't listen, it's not your fault, it will never be your fault.

You will find love and lose many times on your road to womanhood. As you get older, you will be surprised how many will love you. Cherish that love. You will find that you're interested in forensics. You will go to college to learn all about it. You want to become a Crime Scene Investigator. You will find out you're too old for the Police Academy.

I also want to say trust in your intuition, you have a strong and true inner voice. Trusting in yourself is your biggest challenge. Finally, when life gets too hard, just pray and talk to God.   He will listen.

NALA

Small mix breed dog
Her color is sable
Loves getting baths, nails are really long
scratching.

BROTHER

In Philippines
Typhoon destroyed his home
Rebuilding now, home almost done
Happy

CLEVELAND

Where I was born
Didn't like the winters
Cold, wet, snow, slushy, cars sliding
Bye

EULOGY TO JACQUELINE BUTLER

Jacqueline, Jackie, Grandma, Grammy, or G-ma as she was called by the many people and family that loved her over the years of her life. She was born in the winter of 1949, to John and Nellie Whitfield. She was the oldest of four children, brother John Jr., sisters, Sandra, and Vennie. I, Brenda, have been friends with Jackie since we were seven years old. I remember a time when we were in the apartment they lived in, their father was at work and their mother was in the kitchen. We told her mother we were going out to slide on the ice. Jackie's mother told us, "Even if you fall and break your neck, I'm not coming out there." Wouldn't you know Jackie fell and knocked herself unconscious, and she wasn't sliding, she was coming from the store that was below their apartment. She finally opened her eyes and went and sat on the steps. No one went to get her mother because she had said not to come get her. When Jackie went into the house she was crying and lay down and went to sleep. By the time her father came home, we had told her mother what had happened. Her father couldn't wake her up, so he took her to the local hospital. She had a slight concussion. She said to me the next day, "That was the best way to get to stay out of school."

Jackie graduated from Shaw High School in 1968, she didn't go to college until the 2000's. In 2008 she got a diploma in Forensic Science Technology, majoring in Crime Scene Investigation Specialization. But when she was almost finished, she found out that she would have to join the Police Department to do this and be a policeperson for two years before she would even be considered for a CS I position. By this time, she was too old to go into the police academy. She just loved Forensic Science so much that she finished the course, and she would watch TV shows that had everything to do with Forensic Science.

Jackie married her first husband in 1969, by then she already had two children. During this marriage she had two more. This marriage lasted twenty-one years and ended in divorce, but during this marriage they moved to Griffin Ga. where she raised her children, two boys and two girls, who were the light of her life. She told me many times about how she loved all of you, and how you overcame your problems and made a good life for yourselves and your families. Her children also blessed her with 13 grands and 15 great-grands. Her next marriage was in 2004. Those last six months, she said "nope" and walked away. But she was there for her second husband when he was really sick and needed her help. She did what she had to do to get him back to good health and after that she walked away again. She was there for him when she didn't have to be.

Jackie met so many of you here from working with her, at Sybil Mills where you made Sweatshirts and Tee-shirts, and at Nacom where she was an inspector, I have known Jackie for over 70 years since we were in elementary school together. That's really a long time ago. She was just like a sister to me since I didn't have any. We all knew how she was a kind and loving person who would help in any way she could. She loved to travel. She told me her favorite trips were when she went on a seven-day cruise to Alaska with her sister Vennie and four of her friends, and to Dubai and India, going to the tallest building in the world the Burj Khalifa and going to the 124th floor and looking out of the windows at the beautiful city of Dubai. In India to the Taj Mahal, although she had gotten sick from the heat there, she did see the beautiful outside of it and the monkeys running around. My favorite memory of Jackie is how she was there when I had back surgery; she was there to make sure I took my meds. She would cook my food and make sure I made it to my doctor's appointment and was there at every therapy session too. That's why I love her like a sister.

She was the kindest and most loving person you would ever meet. I just want to say to Jackie.

God saw you getting tired,
and a cure was not to be,
So, HE put His arms around you
and whispered, "Come with Me"
With tearful eyes we
watch you fade away.
Although we loved you dearly,
We would not make you stay.
A golden heart stopped beating,
Your hardworking hands put to rest,
God broke our hearts to prove to us
He only takes the best.
Love, you, sister and Rest in Peace, Jackie.

TIME LOST

On a cold night in January,2023 a young couple was walking through Central Park just talking about their upcoming wedding. The wind was blowing but they were in love and didn't even feel it. All of a sudden, there was a glowing swirling light coming towards them. They tried to run but it caught them and pulled them in. Everything looked so beautiful, something they had never seen before. They thought that they were just in the swirling light for just a few minutes, but to their surprise when they returned to the same place in the park it was now ten years in the future. When they looked at each other, they were confused. They were wearing clothes that they couldn't imagine wearing and strange looking. But as they walked through the park there were tall buildings where there had not been before. Missing posters all worn and faded on the trees, but they could see that the faded pictures were of them. They could barely read the words on it, "have you seen Anthony Green and Tasha Andrews missing since January 2023." They looked at each other in disbelief and fell to the ground.

LAST THANKSGIVING IN GEORGIA

The day started out with me feeling happy knowing I would see all my children today, Nov. 25, 2021. Thanksgiving Day, but as it got closer for me to go to my daughter's house, I started feeling sad, knowing that this will be the last Thanksgiving I'll spend with them for a while, because I will be moving to San Antonio Texas to live with my sister.

When I arrived at the house there was the smell of good food cooking. There were four of my great-grands there, when they saw me they all ran and gave me a big hug. My daughter came and told me that my youngest son and his family would not be there because he had to work. Later I heard them saying that he's known for a while, he could have gotten off.

Just then Shaq called me to the kitchen to show me what he had cooked. This was his first time cooking an all plant-based meal, he's eating plant-base food because he has Crohn's disease, and he changed the way he eats, this helps him a lot in keeping a healthier eating habit. While I was scanning the table looking at the potato salad, collard greens, fried turkey and the red velvet cake my daughter made for the first time, I notice something that was supposed to be mac & cheese, for some reason it didn't look right. "Who made the mac & cheese I asked?" A couple of people shouted, "your son." At that moment I thought of the movie Who Made the Potato Salad, and just like that movie where no one ate the potato salad no on ate the mac & cheese.

After everyone had eaten it was time to take pictures, because I wanted memories of that day. The first was of me and three of my children, and it went on with me my children and their spouses, grandchildren, great-grands, and step-grands. After the pictures were taken, I noticed no one was watching football, they were all trying to spend that time with me. Well, it's getting dark and time for me to leave, after hugging everyone goodbye and they were walking me to my car, my oldest son said, "Wait a minute, who told you that you can move to Texas?" Everyone was laughing because he was acting like a small child, and he's 53. "You did at my 70th birthday party I told him. You also said that you had some big black garbage bags I could use." With that I got in my car and went home.

FRIDAY NIGHT ADVENTURE

It was on Friday afternoon when Laura, Patrica, Kelly and Wanda decided that they were going out that night and having some fun at Club Jupiter. By nine pm they were all dressed to kill. They met at Laura's house so they could ride to the club together. That Friday night was so beautiful with the stars shining so brightly in the sky.

They arrived at the club and started mingling with some of their friends that were there too. The music was on point, and they were on the dance floor until the sweat had permeated through their blouse so you could see the color bra they were wearing. After all the dancing they decided that they were going to get something to eat. The nearest restaurant was a Jamaican restaurant that was supposed to have great jerk chicken. After placing orders, they went to the nearest table and sat and waited for their food. There was a conversation going on about what happened at the club when the waitress came to the table with their food, it looked so good. Patrica told the waitress thank you and began to eat. After a couple of bites there was a strange look on their faces. Kelly yelled out, "this chicken is atrocious, get the manager, this meat is old, probably from last week, it has a sour taste." When the manager reached the table Laura explained what was wrong with the chicken. The manager is from Jamaica, and he was talking so fast that Wanda had become bewildered and didn't know what to say or do next.

After they left the restaurant and went over to the Sunshine Mall, which is open all night, to do some shopping, yes, it's two in the morning but that's the best time to shop, the stores aren't crowded. Patricia found a jade Elephant and warrior that she really liked, she went to the owner of the store to asked about the validity of the items, she was making sure they were really jade before she bought them. Two hours later they finally got tired, and a lot of money had been spent. The four made their way back to the car, that's when Wanda yelled, "Wait I forgot my crackerjacks."

PACKING MY CLOTHES

Thrill is gone
Didn't last too long
Six months to be exact
When I started to go pack

What started out as a beautiful love affair
Turned into my worst nightmare
Knew this gentle giant for over 30 years
I also knew his wife, what a sweet woman she was

October 3rd, 2003, is when the downfall started for me
The cussing, drinking, and calling me names,
Is he really talking to me
Honey, fix me something to eat
Grabbing my purse and books and hitting the streets

The thrill is gone, you done me wrong
So along you'll be, I won't be around
Packing my clothes, moving on

MONIQUE COGBURN

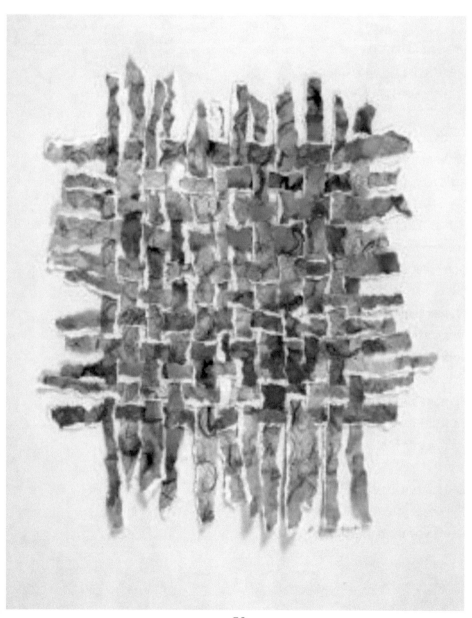

THIS WORLD IS AWESOME

God is hovering.
The universe and darkness.
I love the concept.

On second day, He
Creates the sky and water.
Greenhouse is in place.

Let dry land appear.
Gathering waters were seas.
A playground for all.

Lights: Sun, moon and stars.
The two huge lights: day and night.
One great and one less.

Waters teem with fish.
Abundant living creatures.
Birds flying so high.

Humans and creatures...
Be fruitful and multiply.
Love action is blessed!

God said I will rest.
The seventh day is Holy!
Thank you from us, Lord.

IT BEGINS
AMERICAN SIGN LANGUAGE

In the late 1980s, my husband, my daughter and I attended MacArthur Park Church of Christ. This church had a Deaf Ministry led by two teachers – a married couple. These two had met in college and both aspired to be sign language teachers. His name was Kit. I do not remember her name.

A little bit about my husband James. He would help anybody. Anybody.

One Thursday night at around 9:00 p.m. we got a call from Kit. He said, "James, we need to borrow your truck." James said, "No man. Have to work tomorrow." I told James to hand me the phone.

Kit explained he was moving some deaf individuals into the Light House. I said, "Okay, where can I meet you." We met up and started loading the trucks. I can remember that evening because at midnight those individuals were just signing, giggling, and looking over at me. Kit just smiled.

I can remember this, too, because Sunday morning about 10 to 12 of those individuals accepted Christ and were baptized. I sat there in amazement.

After the service, I looked over at Kit who said, "You just never know, Monique."

Fast-forward to when I attended Bandera Road Community Church (BRCC). There was a signing person there who led the Deaf Ministry. She offered to teach an eight-week course for congregants. I enrolled and I liked it a lot.

In 2019, at one of my Bible studies, I mentioned this story and the fact that I didn't even know if the Lighthouse was still in existence. There was a therapist in my group, and she said, "Yes, it is." I said, "wow.'

And in the last couple of years, I have seen where Northside ISD offered this class as Continuing Education. I was able to enroll in it this semester.

What a fun first day we had! The instructor had me sign that I am happy. When I finished, she said, "Use more expression, please."

It is going to be very interesting to learn this "in-your-face" language.

And I really should change the title to ASL - A Visual-Gestural Language.

The Year Was

1977.
I was graduating from Roosevelt High School on the northeast side of San Antonio, Texas.
Our Valedictorian was 17 years old.
A young black man.
He had received a four-year scholarship to MIT (Massachusetts Institute of Technology).
Impresses me to this very day!

LET ME TELL YOU

It was the year 2013 while I was shopping in a discount department store in Griffin Ga. I came across this picture in the section where pictures are sold. I would always go there to look for pictures because this store sold the pictures you could not find in Walmart's. This store's name is Rose's. It is not quite as big as Walmart's, and its busy time is during the Thanksgiving and Christmas Holidays, and the January sales. It was during that time when I saw this picture.

As I stood there looking at it, memories came flooding back to my brain. The oldest one is me, the one who is whispering something in the ear of the oldest is Sandy, and the younger one is Lynne. Every time I looked at it, I would think about the fun we had playing in the backyard of the apartment we lived in, and the rock throwing fights we had with the kids who lived on the other side of the fence. Running and sliding down the hallway when our mother wasn't around. The elementary school was across the street so we waited until the first bell would ring before we went to school, how the playground equipment was on concrete, no grass or dirt nowhere, and no one died.

Our apartment was above a Ma and Pops store, and we would go down there to buy penny candy. At that time if you had a dime, when you left you had one of the small brown paper bags full of candy. There was an ice cream stand on the other side of the building next to ours, when it was open in the summer we would go every other day for an ice cream cone. One of the memories I remember the most is going down the long flight of stairs to reach the outside. One day we were going out, we were walking down the stairs and just before we reached the door it opened by itself. At first, we were scared, but has it happened a few more times we said it was a ghost and we named it Charlie.

We had the biggest Christmas tree that always had lots of toys and clothes under it. My father was the only one who worked and there were four of us to buy for. We would always find our gifts before Christmas, so my parents started leaving them at the neighbors. I found out after my father death when we found one of his paycheck stubs he only made sixty five hundred a year, that was the early sixties. No one could live off that now even without any children.

After we grew up and had our own lives to live, we would get together on special occasions or funerals. In 2012 I went to West Palm Beach to take care of Lynn after her brain surgery, in 2014 I came to San Antonio to take care of Sandy after her back surgery that left her in a wheelchair. The last time we were together was on a cruise a few weeks ago. Now this picture hangs on the wall over my dresser, where I can sit and look at it and just imagine what the little girl on the left is whispering in her sister's ear. Is she telling her a funny joke or just saying I love you.

IMELDA COOPER

TIME

Lately with so much time in abundance, which is quite rare due to our current sad circumstances, it would be nice to stop and reflect on it. Its pure and simple existence is being overlooked. It's all around if we just pay attention and give it some thought and the value it rightly deserves.

It cannot be seen but its existence can be recognized just by looking in the mirror to see its passing and the changes it has unmistakably made to each and every one of us.

It cannot be savored like the sweetness of chocolate or freshly baked bread or a glass of fine wine. But the memories created and shared with loved ones are delicious.

It cannot be touched, but it can certainly be felt especially when it runs out. When we're busily involved with things or people that we love, suddenly we're left with the desperation of wanting more and more time.

It cannot be heard as one hears music or laughter, but more readily the tic toc of the clock sitting and smiling at one's desk a constant reminder to hurry up and move.

It cannot be smelled literally, but a special scent can most certainly carry you back to times of many moments of great happiness or deep and desperate sadness.

Sadly, it can run; it can fly when we need it most; and, would you believe, it can even stand still if you're quiet and simply listen. So, enjoy this gift of time that has been given to each and every one of us. As we all know too well, it will be gone in the blink of an eye.

CHILDHOOD – COMING AND GOING

About 60 years ago my beloved family and I made the long, long journey traveling across one of the largest states in the US. Looking back on our long, long travel, it really was quite an adventure.

My family endured three years during summers and winters going to Vernon, Texas and coming back to Eagle Pass.

I didn't know then and I still don't care to know today the exact mileage of those dreaded trips. I can only testify that those trips were not exciting.

Just image crossing one of the biggest states in the U.S. from literally one end to the other in an old Plymouth station wagon with 2 adults and 8 kids!

By today's standards it is mind blowing. Imagine having no cell phones, no I-pads or DVD players. We had only each other to talk to or make up some kind of game. We tried counting cars or identifying them but after a while of total boredom it was just easier to fight and that was more fun too. On our very first trip we had barely driven into Del Rio which is about an hour from Eagle Pass, that I asked my father the famous question; "Are we were there yet?" in Spanish of course, "Ya llegamos?". Little did I know we had about 10 more hours to go. But we made it.

Many times, we were simply ecstatic when we actually made it all the way with no flats or the engine not overheating. WOW!

Stops were only made for necessary stuff like gas, water, restroom breaks or to check the engine. During these few stops, it was unthinkable to ask for snacks like chips and dip, candies, cookies or even sodas. The response was always the same, "No hay dinero para todos." (Not enough money for everyone) Homemade bean tacos were the standard food/snack combination my mom was sure to make before each trip. Also on these few stops, it was the older kid's duty to do a head count. We certainly didn't want to lose a little Mexican kid in the middle of Texas.

As I look back now, I understand that these long trips were to better our lives just as I'm sure the early frontiers did so many, many years before.

LARRY ENGLE

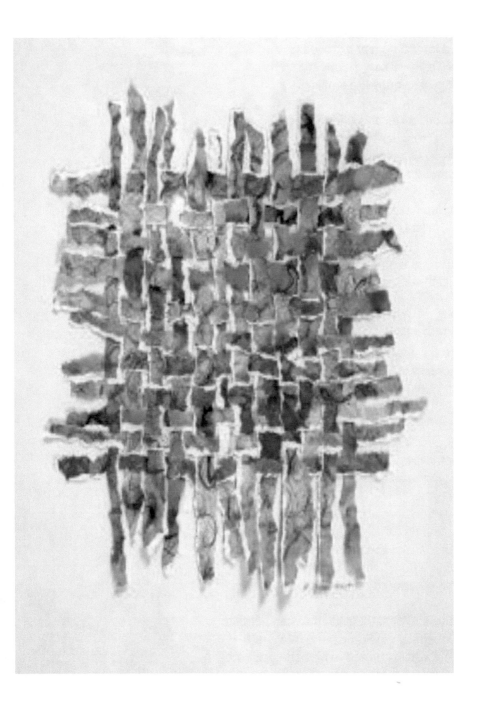

NILE SONG

A thousand oars dipped the Nile
Midst lotus bloom and crocodile.
Upon the royal barge lounged serene
Old Egypt's young Ptolemaic queen.

Jewel bedecked and golden robed,
A dozen tongues she knew and spoke.
Her fleet was launched upon the Nile
To conquer Caesar and beguile.

Cleopatra, a temptress at twenty-one
With Hellenistic beauty seduced Rome's son.
Rolled in a carpet presented as a gift,
Unfurled in her perfume, wearing nothing
But its mist.

Enchantment steeped in the gathering dusk,
A heady brew of spices and musk.
The stars glowed bright in Egypt's skies
As Horus watched from celestial heights.

The fruit of her bosom, a temple her thighs,
Caesar fell captive in the depths of her eyes.
The queen's rival, her brother, was soon
Swept away.
Her every wish Caesar's task, Amun-Ra
Blessed her day.

Thus, the ties of passion tween Egypt and Rome,
Of scandal and spectacle, silver and gold.
Cleopatra bore Caesar his only son,
By this she mused her queendom was won.

No one, she thought could threaten her path
While senators in Rome plotted in wrath.
When Caesar returned to his home for a crown
Assassins gathered to strike him down.

A man one thought nearly a god had died.
Red blood on the steps disproved vain lies.
Cleopatra alone and vulnerable again
Needed a new champion and powerful friend.
Once more the gods favored her graceful hand,
Called to Tarsus, summoned by the man
Who now held power in his Roman grip,
Mark Antony awaited her golden ship.

Again, she set sail upon the Nile,
Diplomacy and beauty mixed with a smile.
The splash of the oars, the hiss of the craft
As it followed the Nile down destiny's path.

Purple sails announced a lavish barge,
Cleopatra's flotilla and entourage.
Mark Antony marveled at this floating dream,
Anxious to share his fiery scheme.

An alliance between her East and his West,
The better to conquer what was left.
Mark Antony's plan was never enough,
It failed to allow for the follies of love.

Soon, he too would fall victim to a queen,
Her radiant countenance, her thin linen's sheen,
The spice of her perfume, a hint of paradise,
The music in her voice, those capturing eyes.

First, there was lust, then love, now treason born,
Against Rome flamed war, the blaring martial horn.
Antony rode in grandeur with his legions at first
Until defeat after defeat and then the worst:

The temptress of men, the nubile goddess not found,
She had left him alone, no more the sound
Of sweet music from her encouraging words,
Only moans of the dying plainly heard.

Cleopatra had fled to a sheltering tomb
To plan her own fate, to control her own doom.
Mark Antony forsaken in a field of gore,
Heartbroken, dejected, fell upon his own sword.

The tale of two lovers who gambled and lost,
Who dreamed of conquest no matter the cost.
Well-worn as the pyramids, the tale still told
Of a goddess queen and her hero, handsome and bold.
Brave deeds are remembered on incised walls,
Glowing murals were painted in hallowed halls.
Mighty columns still rise on Egypt's sand
And colossal kings in stone survey the land.

Here and there maybe, a dusty bronze coin
Portraying the fruit of Ptolemy's loins,
A woman so beautiful yet many would die.
Visions of an empire would end with a serpent
And a sigh.

AZTEC GOLD

Heaven stands before me
In her robes that touch the floor
With tawnsome doe-eyed beauty
Behind the rustic door.

She is my only treasure,
The wealth I hunger to hold,
Lineage dressed in Maya jade,
Adorned with Aztec gold.

A niece of Moctezuma,
A daughter of Kukulcan,
Dark eyes a gentle fire,
Her touch my healing balm.

Jet hair cascades in glory
Streaming thick down her back.
I breathe deep her scent
Knowing all too fully that

I could never leave her,
My rose and copper love,
Her little hands at the comal,
Song learned from a dove.

Los venados of the forest,
El tigre of the night,
The deer her tender kisses,
The jaguar, passion's might.

The days seem quick in passing,
Earth and tears follow the sun.
Though we eventually wither,
I'll praise till life is done.

Beyond stars I want forever,
Beyond dreams this dream to hold.
I have touched Maya jade,
Won Aztec gold.

THE CACHE OF SILVER

Yes, I loved her, how I loved her
As witnessed by the sun
Where nopales grow thick and tall,
Where arroyos seldom run,
Far from grimy cities
That fester in their heat
In a drowsy little village
Where strangers seldom meet.

I was a dusty fugitive just riding through
On a pilgrimage to nowhere
Undecided what to do.
I saw her by chance and dared
Ask her name.
She blushed a bouquet of roses
Asking me the same.
She told me of a livery
And where to find a room.
Saddle bags filled with silver coins
Soon caused my life to bloom.

She worked in a cantina,
The only one in town,
A serving girl and orphan,
Indebted, duty bound.
I observed her very closely
When I took my meals.
Evenings fired with tequila
Caused my brain to burn with zeal.

Innocent as snow she seemed,
Modest as a dove,
I bought her freedom with some silver
And she became my love.
I planned out our future,
And made her my wife.
The priest blessed the ranchito
To start our rural life.

From the cache of silver
Came cattle and other needs.
We built a shelter of adobe
While I forgot past deeds.
Armed with repeating rifles
And six-guns at our side,
Mounted on rugged horses,
To town was a desolate ride.

Our happiness was meant forever,
This would be just another day,
But when we arrived at the village,
My lost past got in the way.
Three grim horsemen were waiting.
When they saw my face,
I spun my horse around,
My wife joined in the race.

We thundered through the village
Scattering the hapless along the way.
If we could just reach the adobe
Was all that I could pray.
Our pursuers were relentless,
Firing round after round,
My poor wife's horse stumbled,
Rolling on the ground.

I reined in savagely, racing
To her side.
She was already dead,
Escape would be denied.
I stood up calmly, faced the
Horsemen as they came
And coldly killed them one by one
As if they were to blame
For my past deeds of darkness,
For stealing the silver horde,
With no remorse in my heart,
What was right or wrong ignored.

Gunsmoke filled the air
With its sulfuric breath.
I looked to my pale wife,
Even beautiful in death.
I buried her at our cabin
Beneath caliche and stone,
Took our guns, my clothes,
The silver that remained,
But did not ride away alone.
All my days I see her
And during the night as well.
Hopefully, she'll stay with me
Till I ride through the gates of hell.

DEVOTION

Once more I keep watch, a dismal specter
Under the mantle of darkness
While owls proclaim their misery,
Perched upon bare branches
In their nocturnal sovereignty
While she sleeps undisturbed
In the cold marble edifice
That defines her refuge.

With one hand I clutch my cloak,
The other rests upon the pommel
Of the sword at my side.
The night wind sighs and groans.
I answer back in kind.

I've known Winter's mocking cold
Though now never feel it,
Remembering instead soft warming lips,
Still, the warmer flesh.
Two hearts want entwined anew
Though a cruel void separates us.
Till the sun rises,
I shall watch patiently,
Then fade, fade away,
Waiting again to be her dark sentry.

SUCH A GOOD MAN

We kissed those first kisses
So tenderly, reverently,
Later kisses with a hungry devouring
Passion as if young, again and again.
At last, I rejoiced,
We are more than just friends.
We went places, she and I,
In a mist of Chanel
Neath our own Van Gogh sky,
Dances and dinners, romantic trysts,
From me pastel roses,
From her little gifts
And she told me,
"You're such a good man.""
All the trappings of a love sublime.
Fool of fools, I dared dream she was mine.
Then came that dark day
Under God's great sun
When she calmly announced
I wasn't the one.
Not the one she had been hoping for,
Not the one to share her door,
Still, all-in-all, I was "such a good man."'
The little farewell speech
Delivered as planned.
"Yes, I know," I laughed,
"I've heard it all before,"
Word for word actually,
As I marched for the door.
"Well, thank you for everything," she said,
"We're still friends."'
"How wonderful," I murmured,
Accepting the end.
I stumbled away with no more said,
No pride left, wishing just to be dead.
Oh, but I was such a good man.
I drove away cursing life and my hex,
Not giving a damn about what came next.
The days that followed gnawed with pain,
Obsessively, I reviewed my lot,

How to judge blame.
I've thought of calling her now and then,
After all, she had said we're still friends
And I was such-a-good-man.
Like an old gray dog that begs a bone,
A phone call at least since I'm always alone.
Still, I hold back in my life's dreary rain,
Filled with misgivings I can only explain,
Once you've tasted the honey
And felt so alive,
It's hard to stay away from the hive.
Though I live to a hundred
I'll never understand
The good in my being such a good man.'

MURDER!

"What'll it be," the caretaker said,
"Murder, romance or a haunting?"
"Murder!" came the reply, eagerly said
For no program was the least daunting,
'I'll turn it to the channel you love,
Where malice and mayhem rule.
When you tire and have had enough,
You can nap in your chair with the stool.
"I'm off to do errands," the caretaker said,
"Be back in just a few....
Back before you too are dead,
Cause murder's against the rule."

ELIZABETH FEHERENBACHER

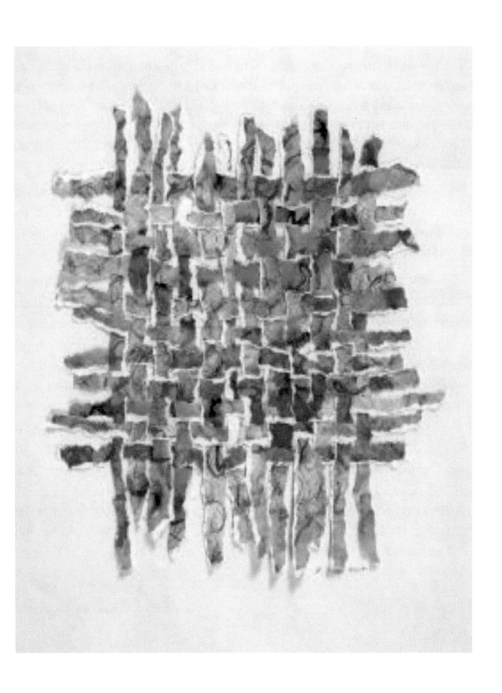

FOND MEMORY OF
A HIPPPY BOYFRIEND

My father was an interesting character, he was very mischievous and a lot ornery. I was on holiday in college and a distant relative (aunt on my dad's side), Pat, was visiting. Pat was known to be a prankster, so sitting around the table with my family, we decided to pull one on her. We decided to have my father pretend to be my college hippie boyfriend. We felt this was the way to go, because their family was so straight-laced.

To put our plan in place, we borrowed my sister's dark long-haired wig and furry vest for my father to wear. Then we added a goatee using eyebrow pencils and eye shadow. Lastly, we handed him some sunglasses and a guitar. He was ready to go.

We called my aunt and told her my boyfriend unexpectedly came to town, and I wanted to come over to introduce him. My aunt was thrilled and interested in meeting my beau.

My dad played his part perfectly, playing shy and speaking very little and then in a low register. My aunt and Pat met us in the kitchen, then we went into the living room where my uncle (my dad's brother) and Pat's husband were seated. My uncle wouldn't look at my "boyfriend". He got up, said something under his breath and left the room. At this point I wasn't sure how much longer I could continue the charade!

We went back through the kitchen with my aunt and her sister to leave and dad took off his wig and removed his sunglasses. Everyone burst out laughing! His brother heard all the laughing and had to come out to see what was happening. He stood there dumbfounded to see his brother laughing heartily because he was able to so prank his family.

SALLY GAYTAN- BAKER

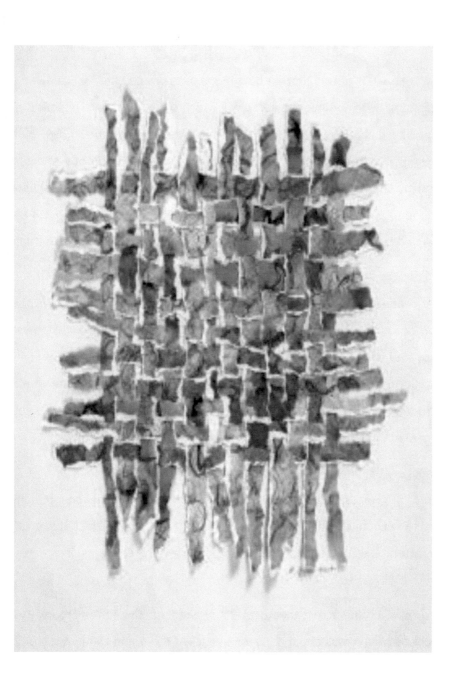

BRING IN THE CLOWNS/
SEND OUT THE CLOWNS

When I was six years old my mother bought me a clown costume for Halloween. The outfit came with a rainbow-colored wig which she combed into pigtails that stuck out like elephant ears. The plastic mask had a large ruby nose, blue eyebrows, and a permanent grin with oversized teeth. For floppy shoes, I borrowed my cousin Nick's size 9 Converse. Mom stuffed them with newspaper and told me to pretend I was marching when I walked so I wouldn't trip. On my wrist she tied two yellow balloons and off we went in search of candy and other goodies.

Everyone remarked how cute I looked and as I stomped my way through the neighborhood. I decided this is what I would be when I grew up: a clown. Clowns are happy and witty. They make kids laugh. They know how to make animals out of balloons. Clowns can wear silly clothes and make-up. No one thinks they're rude when they stick out their tongue and dare you to catch them if you can. It seemed like the perfect job.

As a teenager, I collected clowns of all types, mostly cheerful colorful ones. I discovered a professional clown school existed and that people actually "studied" to become clowns with opportunities to travel worldwide. But soon all was forgotten. I was too busy with more immediate concerns like dates, boyfriends, the Beatles.

One afternoon, I came across the novel "It" by Stephen King at the library. The inside cover stated it was about a clown. I checked it out and thought it would make an interesting read. The story centers around a shape-shifting entity who takes the form of a clown named Pennywise. Pennywise lives in the sewers and preys on young children. He's a scary clown with sharp jagged teeth, phlegmy red eyes, and long razor-sharp nails which extend from claw hands. Every so many years he appears ready to rip little ones to shreds and devour them.

The story frightened and terrified me, but I couldn't put it down. I stayed up all night reading the novel. Afterward I tried sleeping but couldn't. Every time I closed my eyes, I saw the menacing face of Pennywise. And when I opened my eyes, I saw my clown collection, smiling at me with an evil grin. My love affair with clowns ended that night, destroyed by Stephen King and his imagination. The next day, I avoided eye contact with the clowns as I packed them in a cardboard box and donated the collection to Goodwill.

DELICADA

Delicada, my Christmas Cactus, lives on the screened porch at the back of our house. Its succulent flat leaves branch out and spill over the clay pot with the bright sunflower painted on it. A gift from my mother, the glazed pot travelled from Mexico some twenty years ago. The cactus was planted in it two years ago. Bought at a discount sale at Rainbow Gardens, the plant was small, about 4 inches tall, and a little shriveled. It was marked down to a dollar fifty, and having seen pictures of the beautiful flowers it blooms, I decided to buy it.

When I brought it home, Myles shook his head and told me it probably wouldn't survive my care. Several of my house plants have withered and died because I forget to water them. "This is a plant that requires special attention," he said. "If you don't care for it properly, it won't bloom. And if by some miracle, it does bloom, it's only twice a year—Christmas and Easter."

The first year I kept it outside in a cool corner away from indirect sunlight and watered it once a week. It didn't grow much and didn't bloom. I read that a cup of black coffee would help the plant grow. So once a week I poured a cup of coffee into the soil. The coffee seemed to help and the second year, the plant exploded and grew 10 additional green stems. In anticipation, I searched for buds on the tips of the leaves. But in December, I once again accepted defeat— another no bloomer year.

In October of this year, I noticed tiny buds were growing on several of the leaves. Then 2 weeks ago, I saw that, overnight, the first bud had bloomed into a vibrant red bell-shaped flower. There are at least 15 small buds growing on the cactus. I hope by Christmas, it will be in full bloom, ready to celebrate in holiday red. I think of how it took Delicada 2 years to fully blossom—a late bloomer—just like me.

SHADES OF ORANGE

Recently I was thinking about my younger self and how the color orange is interweaved into several of my memories.

My mother would often serve Tang on ice with bacon and egg tacos for breakfast. My brother and I did not care for the taste of the powdered orange flavored drink. But Mom usually convinced us to drink it by telling us it was what smart people like the astronauts drank.

On slow days when I was bored, I would munch on a crunchy carrot in front of my brother and repeatedly say "What's Up Doc?". I knew it bothered him to hear me say it over and over. He would stomp out of the room, threatening to tell mom. This was not a threat to take lightly. Mother had a habit of spanking with a thick leather belt if we misbehaved or annoyed her in some way.

Dreamsicles were my favorite treat on a summer day. The popsicle with a creamy vanilla center is covered with an orange flavored ice coating. It had to be eaten quickly before it melted and trickled down your hand. My brother and I were allowed to walk down the block to the corner neighborhood store where Mr. Salinas, the owner, let us purchase the pops even if we were a few cents short.

My grandmother's sweet potato empanadas were the best. The whole house smelled of cinnamon and nutmeg when she baked these. I would sit outside on the porch, coloring on my color book, eagerly awaiting the sound of the oven door opening, and my grandmother's voice telling me the first batch was ready to eat. Her baked sweet potatoes were also a favorite. Topped with a dab of butter and a drizzle of blackstrap molasses, we would eat them as a snack or part of a meal.

My mother's favorite sundress had large vibrant orange tulips on it. She wore it often and it always put her in a good mood. She would turn on the radio to some bouncy ranchera music and twirl around the room, laughing and encouraging us to dance. My brother and I would dance around her cumbia style.

There was a time when grocery stores only carried seasonal produce. My aunt lived on a farm and when cantaloupe season came around we would eat it every day because once the season ended, we had to wait another year. I remember we had cantaloupe at every meal.

Nothing beats a Texas sunrise in Port Aransas. Vibrant shades of orange and red cast an energizing glow on the land and promise another day of warmth and sunshine.

One of my college courses required the class to watch the movie "A Clockwork Orange." Filmed in 1971, it is based on a novel by Anthony Burgess. The movie takes place in futuristic England and is one of the most disturbing movies I have ever seen. With all that is happening today I sometimes wonder if we are moving toward a Clockwork Orange future. Some in our society seem determined to return to what they call "the good old days" and repeat the dark periods of our past.

CHOCOLATE LOVER

One of my favorite confections is the classic Hershey's chocolate candy bar. I prefer the plain bar without the nuts. I cannot remember the first time I tasted one, but it's been a good friend of mine for a long, long time. The dark brown wrapper with the huge silver-grey letters makes it easy to spot on store shelves or vending machines. I've never had a problem locating a Hershey bar when my craving for chocolate needs to be satisfied.

This tasty concoction has been with me through thick and thin. If I'm sad, happy, depressed, anxious, nervous or excited I can always count on its dark velvety squares to work their magic. On a good day, I slowly unwrap the treat and close my eyes as the scent of cocoa embraces my nose. I relish the moment I put one or two small pieces in my mouth. I place them one at a time on my tongue and just let them sit there and melt. Savoring the moment, I lick my lips so that the chocolate taste will linger. On a bad day, I rip the wrapper off and take huge bites, swallow quickly, and finish the bar in seconds.

Just about anything tastes better when dipped in chocolate. I like to melt a Hershey bar and dip fluffy marshmallows, crunchy graham crackers, sweet strawberries, even crispy bacon in it. Sometimes, when desperate times call for desperate measures, I skip the melting part, break a chunk off the bar and dip it in red wine. Sounds gross but it gives me the quick fix I need.

BONNIE LYONS

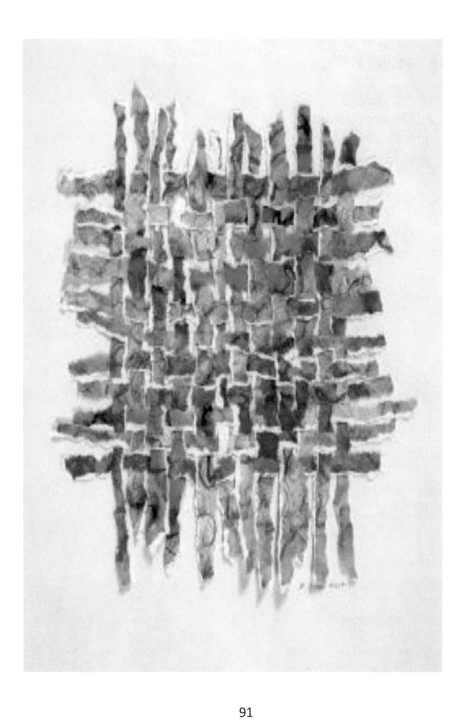

TWO HAIKU:

Wednesday make stuffing
Thanksgiving Day stuff yourself
Black Friday buy stuff.

My neighbors are fine
Their politics are not mine
My neighbors are fine

LUCY POLUDNIAK

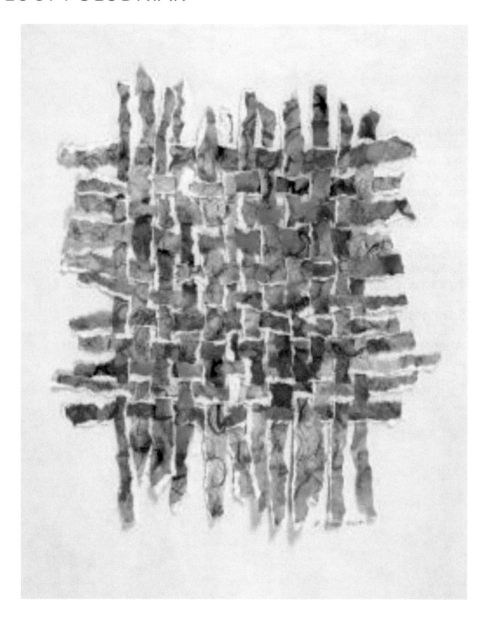

HAIR PINS

Ready to hold in place
fussy hairstyles,
or tame unruly tresses,
or fasten rollers,
or keep in place
pin rolls through the night.

Grandmother's inexpensive
beauty ritual that lasts forever.
Unbending, resolute, untiring.
An inanimate tool providing animation
To a face.

From lone stick to
double pronged warrior: Hair pins.
Weaponizing a woman's crowning glory
in battles for
bobs, twists, flips and beehives
buns, French braids, up dos and knots.

MADMAN ACROSS THE WATER

Energy emanated from his wiry five-foot eight frame
but he could subdue it if required to blend into a crowd.
He had curly blonde hair parted on the side and mischievous hazel eyes
that revealed flecks of copper if you were lucky to catch his gaze.

He wore corduroy jeans with long-sleeved plaid flannel shirts in the winter.
Short-sleeved striped cotton shirts with jeans in the summer.
He smelled of fresh tobacco, a soft-pack Marlboro Reds always in his chest
pocket.
His walk was elvish and devilishly light thanks to his suede Thom McAn desert
boots.

He drove a cinnamon-colored two-door Ford Maverick
And taught me to shift so his hands were free for shaving.
He showed me how to navigate the turns on the Crosstown Expressway
And use the fluorescent highway lines when the fog came in thick.

When Disco Duck played on the Pizza Hut jukebox
We'd laugh and order another pitcher of beer
While waiting for our mushroom, black olive and onion pizza
That imprinted its Mediterranean flavors onto our DNA.

He was bold with questions, pronouncements and poetry
He was curious, empathetic, kind and true
He likened himself to the Madman across the Water
He was my playlist, my core curriculum, my forevermore titan.

OH, FIESTA!

Oh, Fiesta! You wretched, intrusive city-wide party with your boisterous crowds balancing stacks of cups topped with sloshing beer in one hand and skewered chicken in the other.
The hedonistic noise parades down city streets with Sousa-marching high schoolers and troops
and charros and tissue-paper-covered floats carrying the city's elite who deign to show us their shoes.

Oh, Fiesta! You started as a Battle of Flowers by Anglo women in a city known for its Spanish missions--
where insurgent Texicans at the Alamo made their final stand
and their progeny nursed the mythology entered into textbooks as history
and formed the Order of the Alamo to perpetuate castes with a pretend royal court of debutantes.

Oh, Fiesta! Cultural appropriation didn't yet have a name, but my father recognized the farce of Fiesta: Anglo women with paper flowers crowning their hair, wearing joyful, bright colors
in the handcrafted dresses and flowing skirts of indigenous Mexico
while underpaying Maria, their housekeeper and Dolores, their cook.

Oh, Fiesta! When will you confess your racist roots and ask for forgiveness?
When will all your debutantes marry out of membership?
When will the Anglo savior evolve into an ally?
When will the party truly start?

96

THE FRONT

The intermittent gusts slap forcefully through the branches
and down to each leaf that trembles in fright of falling.

With each gust comes the sound of rustling and creaking and moaning
belying the brightness of the bluest sky.

A gust has found me, so I refuge inside sheltering walls with quieting carpet
where now I hear only the tinkling of wind chimes on the porch.

ACCOMPLISHMENT

My greatest accomplishment is surviving.

Counted breath, or mesmerizing chant manages pain.
Measurement of time, day by day, keeps anguish at bay.
An all-in effort, plus wile, outwits want and circumstance.

My greatest accomplishment is surviving.

Grief wrapped its arms around me, tried to smother me.
Illness sapped me physically, secluded me.
Love blinded me, but like Scarlett O'Hara: Tomorrow is another day.

My greatest accomplishment is surviving.

Storytellers inspire me through carefully crafted characters, scenery.
Peers share life's brutal truths, surround me with empathy.
Dogs wake me from nightmares, guard me attentively.

My greatest accomplishment is surviving.

I WAS THE LUCKY ONE

I was the lucky one.
Unlike my two brothers, who as infants were deprived
of his presence by the U.S. Army who needed him
first in Germany and then Korea
before bringing him back to the U.S., but 2,000 miles from home.

I was the lucky one,
because he was with me from the day I was born
and I never felt unloved even when he was again sent overseas
because he'd created memories to sustain me
and wrote me letters and sent little gifts from far away.

I was the lucky one,
with earliest memories of him in khaki green pants
and shirts with sergeant stripes and sewn on name
and laced boots meant to weather place and time—
even décor stamped U.S. Army from a decommissioned base.

I was the lucky one
who rode atop his shoulders and with tiny hands
momentarily covering his eyes, made him laugh
as he guided them back to his chin.
I was the lucky one he had set on top of the world.

DOLORES REYNA

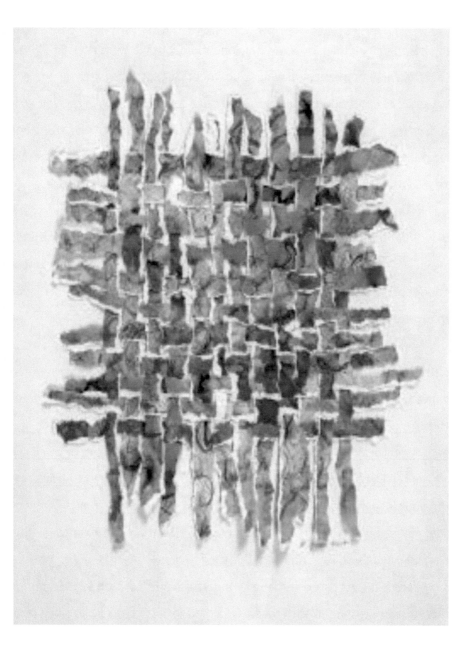

MY LIFE IN FIVE SONGS

You are my sunshine, my only sunshine, you make me happy when skies are gray. You never know dear how much I love you...please don't take my sunshine away. Oh, the innocence of that time when I was ten years old. We had no air conditioner, only one television and only one radio, but we were rich: Six kids all together, playing hopscotch, having club meetings, eating watermelon, and playing baseball till 11:00 o'clock PM so the house could cool down. I bet you golly my siblings remember me singing this song. We ran to the school one afternoon and we found an outside stage. My brothers were going to sit and listen to us. My sisters would be on the stage with me pretending to be singing. Well, there I go using a stick as a microphone and singing you are my sunshine as loud as I could. When we finished there was my dad and other people from the neighborhood looking at us. My dad was laughing and said, "Come down from there before someone reports it to the police for trespassing." To this day I still say this is one of my favorite songs.

When I met my husband forty-eight years ago, I would listen to this artist Rocio Durcal who had this song called Amor Bonito. Throughout all my married life, I have felt that the words in this song apply to the love I have for him. It goes like this. A love like yours is never forgotten. It is not found in the night in a canteen. When I kiss your mouth, I despair. If one day I should miss it, or you leave my side I would be sadly desolate. How nice it is to be with you and realize that without your love it is not worth it. I ask God for you not to forget me, to stay by my side. I love you very much. Hearing this song, I want time to rush to my 50th wedding anniversary so I can dedicate this song to him.

There is a song called "What a Wonderful World" written in 1968 during the time of the Vietnam War. It was performed in the genre of jazz by Louis

Armstrong. It was written to bring hope to the victims suffering the effects of the war. The song says "I see trees of green, red roses too. I see them bloom for me and you and I think to myself what a wonderful world. I see skies of blue and clouds of white. The bright blessed days dark sacred nights and I think to myself what a wonderful world. My youngest son danced to this song with me during the mom and son song during his wedding. Whenever we hear it, we stop and sing it together. In both my sons' lives growing up there have been coach disagreements, girlfriend problems and even softening me to get their dad to give them what they wanted but they learned too that the world we live in can be as remarkable as you make it.

Of course, my life would not be complete without a song for my granddaughters. Anyone ever heard about the Baby Shark song inspired by K bop beats. The song is now a household staple for kids and those kids at heart around the world. We play this song in the car for my toddler granddaughters, to keep them entertained. The part I like is when it talks about Grandma Shark. Just imagine this baby orange shark with brown eyes floating through your screen and there are four of them singing Grandma Shark doo doo doo doo doo doo . There are five stanzas with only those same words. Last week, I called my son and said, "Please play this song for the girls." Immediately, when they heard the song, they dropped what they were doing and ran to the phone. They knew it was their grandma who was doing this for them. Just try playing this music for any child and watch magic being transformed. The song is very catchy.

Looking through my life, I have come to understand that even though my house is now considered an empty nest, there is a new journey coming ahead. Our sons are grown up and have their own families and their own careers. My husband is now approaching retirement and soon he will also figure out what he wants to do with his time. The song that applies to our new old age is by the

Carpenters called," We've only just begun." Words are so applicable to our life

now.

"We've only just begun to live.

White lace and promises

a kiss for luck and we're on our way

we've only just begun

before the rising sun, we fly,

so many roads to choose.

We will start out walking and learn to run and

yes, we've just begun

sharing horizons that are new to us

watching the signs along the way

talking it over just the two of us

working together day today and

when the evening comes

we smile so much of life ahead

we'll find a place where there's room to grow

and yes, we've just begun."

YOU ARE MY SUNSHINE

You are my sunshine.my only sunshine...you make me happy when skies are gray...You never know dear how much I love you...please don't take my sunshine away...

I cannot believe that after so many years I can still remember that as a 10-year-old young girl I loved this song and every time it played on the radio, I would be belting out the lyrics.

Perhaps the lyrics speak of a love that has gone away, the person left behind pleading through troubled dreams for the return of their dearest.

My research shows that Jimmie Davis recorded this song in 1940, and the song prompted him to elected office as Louisiana Governor in 1944. In 1960 he won again, and it became his campaign theme song often singing it while riding a horse named Sunshine.

I know that when I heard this song, it was no man singing it but a woman singer. Come to find out that Doris Day sang it in the 1950's. The only radio we had at home was a white transistor radio that had an antenna and two huge gold dials, one for the volume and the other for tuning to your favorite channel. Sony was the brand, and it only had AM broadcasting at the time. FM broadcasting didn't catch on till the 1960's,

One morning, as we were getting ready to go to school, the song came on the radio. I grabbed the radio and ran around the house singing the song as loud as I could. My brothers would scream at my mom "Mom tell her to stop, she sounds horrible". Dad always made sure the radio had batteries too because he knew all the kids would listen to the radio wherever we went. Oh, the innocence of that time. We had no air conditioner, only one television and only one radio but we were happy. Six kids all together playing hopscotch, having club meetings, eating watermelon and playing baseball until 11:00 pm so our house could cool down. I bet you golly my siblings remember me singing this song. We ran to the school one afternoon and we found an outside stage. The boys were going to sit and listen to us, and my sisters would be on the stage with me pretending to be singing. Well, there I go, using a stick as a microphone, and singing "You Are My Sunshine" as loud as I could. We must have sung it together several times because when we finished there was my dad and several people from the neighborhood looking at us. My Dad was laughing and said, "come down from there before someone reports you to the police for trespassing". To this day, I still say this is my favorite song.

TWO TEN WORD CHALLENGES

While drinking coffee, I was mesmerized looking at a blue wine bottle. Memories flooded in of the healing aspect of my sister-in-law crippled but comfortable in her old age. There had been years' worth of rehab, wheelchair, and canes as well. How she loved her wine, Risotto Moscato sitting on a charger by the table. She could glance outside the window, in satisfaction, watching her garden and, of course, fill a glass to the brim. I wondered how she could waste her time doing this, but now in my old age too, I find myself sitting and just contemplating life. Who is to say I don't need wine too?

I had too much bourbon to drink, Southern Jam, whiskey smash and Kentucky Mule and then ate too much spicy Mexican food which consisted of fajita tacos with mango salsa. This happened Friday night at Norma's house. I realized I was not driving my car home, so I put on my camel-colored wool coat and walked out into the night. I felt frightened of my surroundings as they were eerie. There was a howling sound and the air around me was thick like fog. I felt myself swaying left and right as I walked and realized it must have been the liquor and I almost stumbled onto the ground. Up on a tree branch sat a druid with a pearl earring. Am I witnessing Magic? He had on a navy-blue cape that disguised his appearance and so it was unrecognizable as a human or animal form. He was so huge, and I kept squinting my eyes to see if I could tell how tall it was. Just as I was going to talk to it, it flew like a bird with his wings with a span of five feet wide and disappeared into the sky. Woah, I did have too much to drink!

O BIRTHDAY CAKE

O Birthday Cake
Full of 69 candles
White full of colored sprinkles
Three-layer 10-inch cake with buttercream frosting

O Birthday Cake
Hold on to this age
Do not let time move
Let the vanilla flavor forever last

O Birthday Cake
Gives us all a smile
May this be a joyous occasion
Full of laughter and best wishes

O Birthday Cake
Keep my body suspended
No more wrinkles, saggy body parts
A wish will be said but will not come through if told

O Birthday Cake
Help me blow all candles in one breath
It will symbolize health and vitality
You have become the sign of sweetness and celebrations

O Birthday Cake
for this year, help me lift weights
to build muscle, strengthen bones and improve heart health
Watch my waistline and watch words out of my mouth

GRANDMA

I want to be remembered as a crazy grandma. I do not want to talk about a grandma that gives items away or be considered a woman of old age that represents sickness and fragility. I want to be remembered as someone with strength and an appearance of tranquility, those things that a grandma should possess as a matriarch of the family. Yes, parents give their children things but as a grandma, we always have time, or we always make time that is so vital. I see that my friends have been transformed as generous grandmothers for the good of everyone in the family. Yes, we must remember that we love to wash little bodies, change diapers, feed bottles to a baby but there are other things that make up a grandma. I want to be remembered as the grandma who took the time to make banana pancakes at 3:00 o'clock in the afternoon because her granddaughter wanted it, or I want to wear a motorcycle helmet while washing dishes with her grandson just to make him laugh.

I want to be the grandma that is there to offer money to a grandchild in need, or just because it gives us joy to see them appreciate the spontaneous lunch dates or a treat to the mall. I want to be remembered for the cookie decorating party, the swimming parties and participating in dance parties with the ever-shy Grandson. Grandmas need to live longer to ensure that the next generation lives longer too. We want to enjoy our children, but we want to be asked for permission to take care of our babies. Yes, we understand that you as a young adult mom or dad have running to do but grandparents live in a different rhythm.

We take our time now and enjoy things at a slower pace. I want to be the grandma that has photos and history to tell the life story of the family. I want to be the grandma who has recipes and traditions. Not all grandmas go to college, but they can pass tips on how to do different cooking hacks, Medicinal's and secrets of embroidery. I want to be the grandma that has confidence when secrets need to be told or be able to see in their grandchildren's eyes when they are sad. I want to be the grandma that has general values of sharing creativity of writing, drawing, and cooking. I want to be the grandma that makes and follows a commitment and responsibility of chauffeuring her grandchildren around to activities when asked. And I want to be remembered for constant joy and excitement at decorating for the holidays.

I want to be that grandma that family wants to invite to every important life event because "Grandma has to be there." Our genetic information about personality and sentiments are very much considered when traits in appearance and behavior are seen in grandchildren. Have you heard the following in your family "not only do you look like your grandma, but you act like your grandma, and you are just as crazy as your grandma!" If you have, then you have succeeded as a grandma.

JOANN SANDERSON

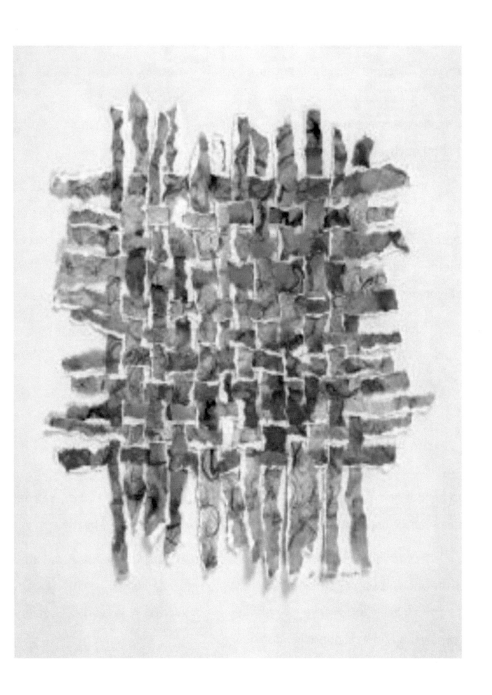

WHEN OPPORTUNITY KNOCKS

If I told you my story "slant," as Emily Dickinson suggests, I doubt you would be sympathetic to my situation. But if you read my story with a discerning mind, I trust you to regard me kindly because I am being honest and have I intent to mend my ways, although you may think I don't show sufficient remorse. You might adopt a "wait and see" stance. But, if you do, at least, you would be giving me another chance.

When my husband, Rodney, told me we had been invited to dinner at the home of the head of Binkman Auditors, LLP, his employer, I was delighted. "Another opportunity," I thought. "But, Rodney, of course, I'll have to shop for something appropriate to wear. Something fashionable but dignified. Something that would impress both Leonora Binkman and her husband."

"Something fashionable, dignified, and within our budget," Rodney replied as he pulled out his wallet and handed me four fifty-dollar bills. "And remember to give me the receipt for our records."

Before Rodney and I were married six months ago, my parents warned me that my profligate spending would cause problems. They reminded me often of my, as they put it, former "missteps" while walking on the wild side during my high school and college years. Mom and Dad looked at each other, worried glances emanating from their eyes as Rodney and I told them our plans.

I assured them I knew Rodney is frugal and persnickety, but now I am a person who knows that problems are invitations to seek solutions. "Don't worry so much. I have a lucrative position as a graphic designer at Go Graphics, Incorporated. I'm a responsible adult now."

Rodney, however, took the first step to avoid rather than solve potential problems. After Rodney insisted, I agreed to close my individual credit card account. However, I intended to find creative ways to modify this restriction. My problem-solving skills are clever and bold rather than methodical and punitive, as are my well-meaning husband's.

Rodney is the firm's newest hire. He is intelligent, persuasive, but is not sufficiently financially compensated for his service—yet. I am determined to help Rodney climb the ladder of financial success. And now this dinner gives me an opportunity to help him take a step forward to becoming a partner in Binkman Auditors, LLP. I am determined, in my soon-to-be beautiful new dress, to charm the Brinkmans.

"Thanks, Dear. I'm sure I'll be able to find something you will like," I looked at the four fifty dollar bills he handed me, "for 200 dollars."

You see, Rodney could interpret tax codes and verify financial statements but did not understand the nuances of networking and the social milieu of auditors. These were my specialties.

Before I set off to select a dress at the moderately priced Xavier's Designer Salon, Rodney reminded me, "You know I want you to look great, but you must stay within the budget. Besides, you look great in anything."

I interpreted his words as a warning ameliorated by a compliment.

The day after he told me about the dinner invitation, I walked into Xavier's Salon wearing tan, straight leg Ponte knit joggers, a white waffle-knit sweater, carrying my cappuccino-colored leather tote bag.

The three salesclerks were helping other customers, so I had time to peruse the offerings, select five items, and take them into the dressing room, although I was interested in only two of them.

I tried on the $180 Susan Elders dusty blue knit fit and flair dress. I decided it was spunky but wouldn't be too threatening to dowdy Leonora Brinkman. Then I tried on the Cassie Lee $420 chiffon dress printed with vertical swirls of cream and grey stripes. This dress looked great on me—sophisticated, yet sexy. Looking directly at my reflection in the dressing room mirror, I defied an imagined Leonora, "Too bad, Leonora, you'll just have to deal with it."

Then I remembered the $200 in my wallet and Rodney's directive. There I was in a dressing room at Xavier's Designer Salon being tested in a trial by fire— a problem inviting an opportunity to solve my dilemma.

I removed the chiffon dress, took the fit and flair to the salesclerk, handed her four fifty-dollar bills, put the $5.60 change in my wallet (I knew he'd count the change), and left the store.

At five o'clock I arrived home, went directly to the bedroom, shut the door, removed the carefully folded $180 dusty blue fit and flair from its box and laid it on the bed. Then I emptied the item in my tote bag—the $420 cream and grey striped Cassie Lee chiffon. As I held it up against my body to admire it in my full-length mirror, I announced, "When opportunity knocks, you must open the door. I am a very savvy partner of a man who will soon be a partner in Binkman Corporation, LLP."

But then I looked at the dusty blue fit and flair lying on the bed. I picked it up, held it against my body, and looked again at my reflection in the mirror. "Wow, this dress is great, too! Maybe I didn't need to jeopardize my future and Rodney's by engaging in this escapade; after all, Rodney and I agree: I look great in anything—anything but an orange jump suit." I laid the dusty blue fit and flair beside the cream and grey striped chiffon on the bed.

As I stood beside the bed looking down at my newly acquired possessions, I heard footsteps outside the bedroom, followed by three soft taps on the door. Rodney opened the door and announced, "I got off early today, Honey. Looks like you've been shopping."

He walked toward the two dresses lying side by side, each with an attached price tag attracting the scrutiny of an auditor's eye. I saw the disappointment in his eyes when he asked me for the receipt. I know he knew what I had done. I handed it to him, and he took it to his office.

And there you have it, reader. This story hasn't ended yet. Rodney is in his office recording my personal assets and liabilities, my strengths and my weaknesses—what I have deposited and what I have withdrawn from the Bank of Marital Expectations. He's doing a risk management assessment. Being savvy and clever, I won't interrupt him.

As for me, I don't have to record anything in a ledger. He identified the problem, as auditors do. But I had already figured out how to solve it just by looking in the mirror.

THIS IS HOW IT BEGAN

The wealthy, widowed business magnate, Josiah Featherstone, had made a will which stipulated that 45% of his assets would go to his son, Horace: 45% of his assets would go to his son, Wilton; and 10% of his assets would go to his daughter, Agnes. If any child died, his allocation would be divided between the two remaining. If two of them died, both their two allocations would be given to the survivor. All his assets would be given to charity if, God forbid, all three of his children would die.

Since Agnes was unmarried, 55 years old, and would most likely never produce an heir, she was satisfied with this arrangement. She had told her father, "My cat, Arabella, and I require a minimum of material possessions."

Over the years, Horace and Wilton began arguing in their mansion on Covington Lake. Each accused the other of manipulating the family's finances to his own advantage. Their arguments were growing louder and more frequent.

One morning the men's vehement voices and the clamorous sounds of thumping, bumping, and crashing from the spacious living room prompted Agnes, tightly holding Arabella, to race down the staircase from their upstairs bedroom to the spacious living room below.

They found the curtains had been torn from their rods, shards of glass from the chandelier lay on the marble floor, sofas, chairs, lamps, end tables had been toppled, and three Tibetan mastiffs were wandering about in circles. Blood stains spotted the rugs, the walls, and the Matisse paintings which had been torn from their hooks , landing willy-nilly throughout the room.

Horace's dead body lay sprawled across one of the toppled sofas, and Wilton's dead body lay on the floor by the fireplace with a poker lying in his open right hand.

Stroking Arabella's fur, Agnes lamented, "Oh, Arabella, so this is how it all ends." She walked slowly around the room, circumventing the bodies and the toppled furnishings. As she walked, she began to smile as she mentally calculated, 45+45+10, 45+45+10.

"No, Arabella, this is not the end. In a short time, you might say, if you could speak, that for us, this is how it all began. Perhaps it is time to call 9-1-1. Such a nice kitty you are."

A TEN WORD CHALLENGE
STICKY SITUATION AT THE STICKY BURR SALOON

Note:

I wrote this account based on my interview with a patron, Colonel W.W. Burns, who was present at the scene the night of this occurrence.

Doc Ambrose Colton

As Blanche Tibbets , the hefty bartender in worn dungarees and plaid flannel shirt, reached for a bottle of tequila on the shelf behind the bar at the Sticky Burr Saloon, she smelled the familiar aroma of Musky Mesquite—an aroma that neither smoke, beer, whiskey, or a month of collected sweat could disguise. She had concocted a mysteriously fragrant lotion in her kitchen, poured it into a 20-ounce pickle jar, and proudly presented it to Burly Bob Mahoney for his birthday a week ago.

Expecting to greet Burly Bob with a discreet peck on the cheek, she turned to see petite, perky, Georgette Dubois, whom Blanche referred to as Miss Curly-Corn Locks, with a broad smile on her pink-painted lips.

"Am I catching a whiff of my specialty lotion—Musky Mesquite—emanating from your pasty-colored skin, Miss Curly-Corn Locks?"

"It short, is Musky Mesquite you're a whiffin,' Miss Blanche? But it ain't no specialty lotion of yours. Burly Bob Mahoney, the cowboy from the Far-Flung

Ranch down the road, done ordered this lotion from Paris, France, to present to me as a token of his affection, admiration, and undying devotion."

"Then, Miss Curly-Corn Locks, you must be talkin' about my Burly Bob Mahoney, the cow poke from the Far-Flung Ranch, whom I lassoed, threw to the ground, branded, broke, corralled, and oiled down with the specialty lotion that I concocted in my own kitchen and thereafter labelled exclusively as Musky Mesquite."

Their eyes locked in a prolonged stare-down. Just as Blanche was about to hurtle over the bar to engage Miss Curly-Corn Locks in mortal combat, Burly Bob entered the saloon, paused, checked out the lay of the land, devised a strategy to ameliorate his present circumstances, sauntered toward them, and obsequiously announced, "Evenin,' ladies."

The curious crowd at the saloon, sensing tension and intrigue, began slowly circling around Burly Bob, Georgette, and Blanche.

Blanche sprang into action, swinging her legs over the bar, splintering three planks of the wooden floor as her crocodile boots made landfall, taking three long strides, before standing smack dab in front of Burly Bob, and shouted, "I ain't about to compete with this prissy, sniveling, fodder-deprived, stringy-haired, toe-painted hussy! And I ain't overly impressed with your taste in fillies or with the workin's of that pea-sized mass hidin' somewhere in your sorry skull substitutin' for a brain."

Blanche and Georgette looked at each other again. But, according to retired Colonel W.W. Burns, who was frequenting the Sticky Burr Saloon the evening of this encounter, reported that this exchange was "conspiratorial, rather than intimidating; subtle rather than obstreperous."

"You've gone too far, Blanche Tibbets," Georgette shouted as she lifted her red crinoline petticoat, reached for a gun strapped to her left thigh, and pointed it at Blanche. In the next moment, she pivoted and pointed the gun at Burly Bob. Then she turned back to Blanche, handed her the gun, and offered, "Here, Blanche. You do the honors."

Blanche pointed the gun straight at Burly Bob's <u>heart</u>, lowered her aim, and shot directly at her target—Burly Bob's right shoulder.

Georgette walked toward Blanche and put her arm around her shoulder. "So, Blanche, how'd you say you made that mighty fine lotion?"

The last words curious patrons at the Sticky Burr Saloon heard as Blanche and Georgette strolled out of the saloon were the first words of Blanche's reply, "Well, I started out with a few drops of ..."

HAIKU NARRATIVE

Monday
I have a great thought,
a pencil and eraser,
but have no paper.

Tuesday
I have a pencil,
a great thought, and some paper,
but no eraser.

Wednesday
I have some paper,
an eraser, and great thought,
but not one pencil.

Thursday
Eraser, I had
and a pencil and paper,
but I lost my thought.

Friday
I had a pencil,
eraser, paper, and thought,
but no time to write.

Saturday
Having pencil, thought,
eraser, paper, and time,
I count, and I write.

Sunday
One hundred nineteen
syllables march on the page—
a haikuist's dream.

TERRI YBARRA

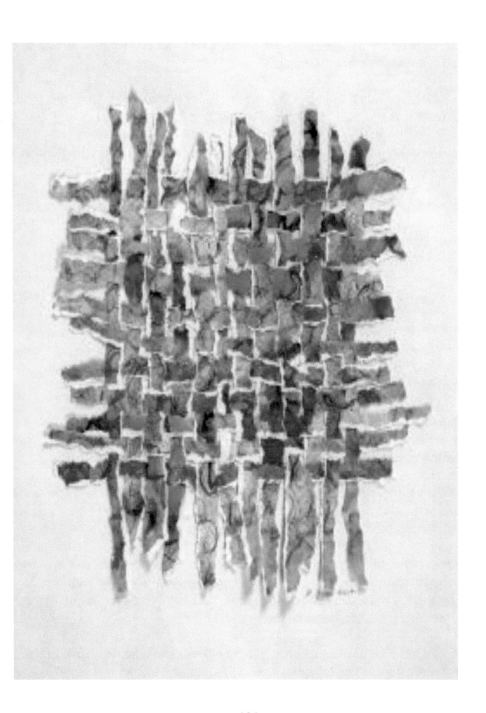

I LOST MY MEMORY

I lost my memory. I think I placed it on the windowsill one winter morning so it could sun. Or was that my geranium?

No. Now I remember. I put it in the middle drawer in the kitchen so no one would mistake it as theirs. No. I think those are my keys.

Okay. Now I remember. I placed my memory next to my bed on the floor so it would be the first thing I put on. Oh no. Those are my chanclas.

I definitely put it away in the closet in the guest room. But isn't that for the out-of-season stuff like coats and boots? My memory is not out-of-season. At least, not yet! Or is it?

I have one other last place where I put things. My attic must have my memory. But I go there only once a year for the Christmas things. I surely need my memory more often!

I don't even remember why I want my memory. I do remember vaguely it being a devilish imp reprimanding me for things I want to forget. Maybe I hid it so I would not remember those times. Nah, can't be that.

But I know my memory is not a physical thing placed in the material world. It is somewhere in my mind connected to a sound or smell or a feeling I once experienced. But it hides from me on purpose still.

When I hear the joyous laughter of my great grandchildren toddlers, I know I have heard that sound before. But when and how and where and who? I want to relive the past happiness knowing it is as marvelous as present sounds.

My memory flitters between hedges in a forest of mazes that record times past, whispering clues in the dark that lead to unrecognizable corridors with electrons that are everywhere all the time at the same time as in a dream. Oh no! That was this morning's conversation with my husband.

Is my memory an opiate that changes the ugly past to a heaven, or is it a wild horse that refuses to be tamed? Either way, I want it back.

Maybe I need to put my raised crossed arms against my forehead and lean on the memory tree, count to ten and play hide-n-seek. What could be more fun than that?
I DON'T REMEMBER!

MISSING?

Christmas is a wonderful time of the year, but it doesn't have crepe myrtles blooming stubbornly or bluebonnets prancing on the highway.

Easter is as exciting, but sage is not perfuming deserts. Nor are prides of Barbados swaying rhythmically in the all too hot wind.

Thanksgiving is delicious even without crocuses or lilies or tuberoses.

Year-round consistency does exist. Every night his hand holds mine gently His arms embrace mine to comfort. His lips kiss mine to remember.

MY TIME

As I look at the road before me, the thorns are gone. The roses remain. No time to wonder if the rocks are there. Just walk and smile or laugh and play.

Instruct no more but learn and giggle. Change diapers, not for me. No work, no clock, no boss, no need. My independence rout does wiggle.

The time has come to have no time. The now is what is left to me.

If now I want to eat and drink, who is to say that it must not be or be?

I plan a thing that is undone, as quickly as I decide as I see fit. To do or not to do is based on what? My wishes, my likes, my mind, my time, my wit!

My time is not as you can see, for now I am a healthy 80 year old.

ODE TO MY WRINKLES

I woke up one morning from what seemed to be a long sleep. The world was the same, but, on inspection, my face was not. It had wrinkles.

Some deep, some shallow. The worried forehead had a few. Around the mouth, like parentheses, they glistened gleefully. Tiny feet radiated from the nearsighted eyes. The sun, the wind, the age left not so hidden on my face marks that lead to memories that complete a life. No creams were ever used on this once smooth, even colored skin of an innocent youth I no longer recall exactly. What adventures marked this face?

School, marriage, child rearing each leaving an indelible indentation on a face that looks more and more like my ancient mother – not in her youth, but at my age now.

I AM ANCIENT!

I worked hard all my life for these wrinkles I now see finally on my face, wrinkles like my mother's face.

WHAT A POWERFUL WOMAN!

I AM NOT PREJUDICED

I am not prejudiced just because growing up I never realized blacks had separate facilities.

No, I am not prejudiced just because I have no black friends.

Of course, I am not prejudiced just because I allow black jokes in my presence. Nor am I prejudiced just because I do not watch movies whose cast is mostly black.

So, what if I was surprised that it was the Japanese army that rescued the world in the Godzilla movies! That doesn't mean I was prejudiced.

So, what if I felt uncomfortable simply because all the people there in Oklahoma were white.

So, what if when I asked what I would call a black man in outer space, I could not think the word astronaut!

So, what if I walked faster as a group of young black men approached me coming out of a mall.

Just because I giggle internally when a creationist asserts that the world was built in seven days.

Just because I balk at all concepts that are different from mine.

I hate piercings and tattoos and orange hair and …, but that does not make me prejudiced.

What's wrong with my wanting everybody to be like me?

That's not why I am prejudiced.

NOT YET

But I'm not dead yet
Balked the elderly woman at the teenager
Who failed to steal her purse.

But I am not dead yet
Explained the old priest
Who advised the sinner
To avoid temptation

But I am not dead yet
Called out the veteran tennis player
To the singles champion
Who could not return his serves.

But I am not dead yet
Shouted the ancient patient
To the insensitive doctor
Who cavalierly spoke of her illness.

But I am not dead yet
Insisted the grandfather
Who could beat any of his
Grandchildren at dominos

But I am not dead yet argued the senior applicant
With the employer
Who did not hire him.

But I am not dead yet
Pleaded the senior neighbor
With the local organization
That she should not be ignored.

But I am not dead yet called out
Wisdom to Inexperience
Who was trying ineffective solutions.

Made in the USA
Columbia, SC
21 November 2024

47011135R00070